THE GLITTERING BLADE

Nate pivoted. Simultaneously, a latticework of limbs part-ed and out barreled the man in the checkered shirt. In his right hand was a long knife. Uttering an inarticulate cry, he leaped, shearing the blade at Nate's chest. Instantly Nate swept up the Hawken, deflecting the blade, and shifted to drive the heavy stock into the man's stomach. But as luck would have it, his foot lost its purchase on a smooth trunk, and the next thing he knew, he was falling.

Somewhere, someone screamed. Nate barely heard them. He slammed onto the wide bole with bone-jarring force, and the world exploded in a riot of bright dots and dancing colors. Struggling to sit up, he shook his head to clear it.

The man was dropping toward him with the knife upraised to cleave his skull in half.

WILDERNESS

Frontier Fury

David Thompson

LEISURE BOOKS NEW YORK CITY

Dedicated to Judy, Joshua and Shane.

A LEISURE BOOK®

December 2001

Published by

Dorchester Publishing Co., Inc.
276 Fifth Avenue
New York, NY 10001

ISBN 0-8439-4949-X

Printed in the United States of America.

Visit us on the web at www.dorchesterpub.com.

Frontier Fury

Chapter One

Out of the heat haze to the west hiked four weary figures. Their clothes were caked with the dust of endless miles and they walked with a wooden stiffness born of sore muscles and fatigue. Behind them was a baked plain. Before them emerald foothills climbed toward majestic peaks.

In the lead strode a broad-shouldered man in buckskins and moccasins. A shock of black hair crowned rugged features distinguished by striking green eyes and a black beard. He was a walking arsenal. In addition to the Hawken rifle he carried, four flintlock pistols were tucked under his wide brown belt. On his left hip was a tomahawk. On his right hung an eighteen-inch double-edged knife with an ivory hilt. Across his wide chest were slanted a possibles bag, an ammo pouch, and a powder horn.

Pausing, Nate King surveyed the foothills and announced, "We'll find water ahead."

"Thank goodness, Pa," said the girl of ten who trudged beside him. "I'm so thirsty I could drink a lake." Attired in a buckskin dress, Evelyn King had Nate's green eyes and her mother's raven hair. "Or a river. I'm not fussy."

The woman behind them laughed lightly. Winona King was a full-blooded Shoshone, a beauty who would turn heads in any village or city on the continent. Her buckskin dress was exactly like her daughter's. It should have been, since she had sewn them both herself. She, too, was armed with a rifle, and had a brace of pistols under a thin belt. Slung across her left shoulder was a possibles bag slightly smaller than her husband's. "How much longer do you think it will take us?" she asked in impeccable English.

"In three days we'll reach the Green River country," Nate said. "If we're lucky, we'll run into some of your people and they'll let us borrow a few horses. In which case we'll be home in less than a week. If not—" He shrugged. "Another eleven to twelve days."

"My people?" Winona said. "They are yours, too. Or have you forgotten you were adopted in our tribe?" she teased.

"How could I forget, dearest?" Nate rejoined. "It was one of the greatest honors ever done me."

The fourth member of their quartet snorted. "You two are enough to gag a spinster. If I'd known I would have to put up with you acting like lovesick sprouts, I'd never have tagged along."

"Who are you kidding, Ezriah?" Nate said. "If it wasn't for us, you wouldn't be on your way back to civilization."

Ezriah Hampton muttered under his breath, a habit when he was annoyed. His wizened face was seamed with wrinkles, each a testament to the scores of years he had lived. His right eye twitched in its socket as he regarded the Kings; his left was stitched with scar tissue, the eyeball long since lost to an Indian lance. He had white hair and a scraggily white beard, neither of which had been combed or brushed in ages.

Hampton's clothes were equally unique. Over a loose-fitting

purple shirt and buckskin pants he wore a red velvet coat with a row of bright brass buttons that gleamed in the sunlight. Over the coat a blue cloak was draped, the collar trimmed with white lace. His footwear consisted of a pair of high-heeled, knee-high black boots. On his head rested a broad-brimmed Spanish-style hat. He had a rifle, two pistols, and an ornate curved sword attached to a belt inlaid with silver studs. A large, finely tooled leather bag was over his right shoulder, his arm wrapped around it as if the contents were valuable.

"Civilization!" Ezriah repeated. "I can't hardly wait! It's been twenty years since those bastards got their paws on me. Twenty damn years! I'd give anything to be able to live them over again as a free man."

Nate didn't blame the old trapper for being bitter. Hampton had been a captive of a tribe called the *Sa-gah-lee*, who recently had taken Winona and Evelyn captive, too. All three would still be in their clutches if Nate had not rescued them.

"You're lucky my pa came to save us," his daughter commented.

"That I was, sprout," Ezriah conceded. "But if I could, I'd go on back there with enough black powder to blow the sons of bitches to kingdom come."

Winona gave Hampton a cross look. "I will thank you not to use profanity in the presence of my daughter."

"So you keep telling me," Ezriah said. "Are you afraid her ears will fall off? Or I'll taint her with my nasty language?" He tittered. "I can't help it. Using cuss words is as natural as breathing. It's how I've always talked."

"Perhaps it is time for you to change, then. A person is never too old to acquire good manners."

Mirth pealed from Ezriah in hearty guffaws. "Only a female would come up with such a fool notion! Manners are for polite society, for prissy sorts who need five spoons just to eat soup." He slapped his thigh in amusement. "You're a living revelation, lady. I had no idea Indian women could be as silly as white gals."

"Tell me, Mr. Hampton. Before you were taken captive, were you ever married?" Winona inquired.

"No, I sure wasn't."

"I am not surprised."

Nate chortled. His wife could more than hold her own in a battle of wits, as the trapper had readily learned. The two constantly squabbled, largely because Ezriah was as ornery as the year was long and as feisty as a randy goat.

The foothills ahead were covered with pines. Higher up firs and stands of shimmering aspens were prevalent. Higher still towered the regal peaks. Nate's gaze was drawn to a notch on a sawtooth ridge, a possible pass over the range to the country beyond.

"Say, Pa?" Evelyn said casually.

"Yes?" Nate absently replied as he pondered the easiest route to reach the ridge. It would take the better part of the day, at least.

"Are there any white folks living hereabouts?"

"Not that I know of," Nate said. Only a few whites called the Rockies home; the number of settlers could be counted on two hands.

"Think there are any mountaineers in these parts?"

Nate glanced down at her. "Mountaineers" was the term mountain men used to describe themselves, and none lived within a hundred miles or better. "I doubt it. Why all these questions, princess?"

"I was just wondering what all these shod tracks are doing here, is all."

Only then did Nate realize the ground underfoot was pock-marked with hoofprints made by horses fitted with horseshoes. He had been so intent on the mountains he hadn't noticed.

Dumbfounded, he sank onto a knee and ran a hand over the impressions.

Evelyn hunkered next to him. "What do you make of them?"

"They're several days old," Nate calculated. "Three riders, heading east as we are. Where they came from is anyone's guess."

"Trappers, you think?" Ezriah asked hopefully.

"It's not likely," Nate answered, not since the beaver trade had pretty much petered out in recent years thanks to a change in fashion back East. Beaver was out, silk was in, and most trappers had taken the hint and moved on to greener financial pastures.

"Soldiers, maybe," Winona said.

Again Nate was skeptical. The closest military post was Fort Leavenworth, far, far off on the Missouri River. Bent's Fort was nearer, although not by much, nestled within spitting distance of the front range of the Rockies. But Bent's Fort, its name notwithstanding, was a trading post, not a garrison.

Ezriah was examining the tracks, too. "Well, whoever it was, it sure as hell wasn't Indians. Not unless they stole the critters from careless whites."

"That could be," Nate said. Some tribes had perfected horse stealing to a fine art. To the Sioux, the Blackfeet, and others, it rated as high as counting coup by striking an enemy with a coup stick. He rose. "It's nothing for us to worry about. Whoever they were, they're long gone by now."

Soon they started climbing, ascending into the foothills, into woodland alive with the chittering of squirrels and the warbling of songbirds. Jays squawked at them from roosts in trees. Chipmunks skittered over boulders and logs. Once several does broke from the underbrush, stared a few moments, then trotted off, their tails raised like black flags.

"Where's that water you promised?" Ezriah asked.

"There," Nate said, pointing at a band of cottonwoods that bordered the base of the next hill. Experience had taught him deciduous trees were partial to waterways, and this time was no exception. Within half an hour they were seated in comforting shade. Winona and Evelyn had dipped their bare feet in a cool, flowing water. Ezriah was a few yards upstream on his hands and knees, gulping nonstop.

Nate settled for a few handfuls, then perched on a stump to keep watch, the Hawken across his thighs. In the wilderness a man couldn't afford to let down his guard. Lapses resulted in violent, sometimes fatal, consequences.

Evelyn, giggling, wriggled her toes. "When we get home the first thing I want to do is take a bath."

Winona's eyebrows arched. "My ears must not be working properly. Since when did you start liking baths? As I recall, you did everything in your power to get out of taking them. Even fibbing on occasion."

"That was when I was little," Evelyn said earnestly. "I'm a big girl now."

Ezriah stopped quenching his monumental thirst to snicker. "Any bigger, gal, and you might be able to beat a possum in a wrestling match."

"Be nice," Winona said sternly.

"I was only joshing," Ezriah responded. "Land sakes, don't Shoshones have a sense of humor?"

"Of course we do. But I do not like having my daughter constantly made fun of."

Evelyn placed a small hand on her mother's arm. "It's all right, Ma. I'm used to him by now. He doesn't mean anything by what he does. Pa says he can't help it. Mr. Hampton just talks before he thinks."

The old trapper's only eye narrowed on Nate. "Is that a fact? Been jawing about me behind my back, huh?" To Evelyn he said, "Any other tidbits your father shared with you, youngster?"

"He says you act meaner than you really are," Evelyn naively disclosed. "Oh. And that you have the most atrocious taste in clothes this side of the divide."

Nate grinned. She had quoted him word for word but she left out a part. "I also said it wouldn't hurt if you treated yourself to a bath, too. As hot as it's been, with all those clothes you have on you're rather ripe." Nate was being polite. The man stunk to high heaven.

"Like hell!" Ezriah declared, and raised his left arm to sniff his armpit. "I like how I smell. Besides, everyone knows baths are bad for the health. They make a fella puny and sickly. I haven't had one in nigh on thirty-five years, and I don't see any reason to break my streak."

Evelyn stared across the gurgling stream. "Pa? Do you suppose the warriors who made the tracks down below came this way looking for something?"

"How's that?" Nate said. He was watching a pair of red hawks soar along the ridge above.

"Aren't those more footprints on the other side?"

Nate was to the opposite bank in four long strides. A patch of mud had been churned by heavy hooves, a single horse this time, the prints only a day old. The rider had let the animal drink a spell, then ridden on up the mountain.

"What do you make of it, husband?" Winona asked at his elbow.

The implications were troubling. "There must be a village nearby," Nate said. "And they could well be hostile." Shoshone country was to the east. To the northwest lived the Flatheads and Nez Perce, both equally friendly. To the south were the Utes, his bitter enemies until recently when a truce was established. Nate was more concerned about running into the tribes belonging to the Blackfoot Confederacy, or the

Crows. The latter had been peaceable enough until about a year ago when a rift developed with the Shoshones.

"Perhaps we should lie low and travel at night," Winona suggested.

"I'd rather not," Nate said. Traveling at night was safer but a lot slower. "If we keep our eyes skinned we shouldn't have any trouble."

Winona patted her parfleche. "We are low on jerky and pemmican."

"We'll get by," Nate said. They had been living off the land, conserving what was left of their meager food supply. But with a village in the vicinity, it would be unwise for him to shoot game. The sound of a shot could carry for miles at that altitude and might draw unwanted attention. "We should be in the clear in a day or two."

"Let us hope so."

They returned to the other side and Nate sank back down on the stump. Hampton was on his haunches, his right hand buried in the large leather bag. A metallic tinkling sparked Nate to say, "Fingering your newfound wealth again?"

Ezriah pulled his hand out. In it were eight or nine gold coins. Spanish mint, part of a secret cache belonging to the *Sa-gah-lee*. "Want to hold one? They're so smooth and pretty. Give me gold over a woman any day. Gold can't sass a man or nag him to death."

In the act of dampening her face and neck, Winona turned. "You are incorrigible, Mr. Hampton."

"I am?" Ezriah blinked a few times. "Is that good or bad?" Without waiting for her to answer, he said to Nate, "How is it your woman speaks the white tongue better than most whites I know? Sometimes I have no idea what she's talking about even when she's talking my language."

"She's a born linguist," Nate proudly complimented her. "She takes to new tongues like a duck to water."

"It helps that my husband has shelves of books in our cabin," Winona said.

"I envy you," Ezriah said. "Me, I never did cotton much to schooling. My father tried his best to force me to learn, but after he wore out five or six switches on my backside he gave up."

"Learning is fun," Evelyn piped in. "If you want, when we get back, I'll teach you how. At your age you should learn quick."

Nate suppressed a laugh at the grizzled oldster's comical expression.

"Girl, I don't rightly know whether I should be flattered or insulted. It's kind of you to offer, but it isn't easy to teach an old dog new tricks."

"Really?" Evelyn said sweetly. "I've never had an old dog, so I wouldn't know."

Exasperated, Ezriah stood. "How much more time are we going to waste flapping our gums? Let's keep going while there's still plenty of daylight left."

For the next couple of hours they climbed steadily. Nate was on the lookout for more hoofprints but saw none. Along about two in the afternoon they stopped to collect their breath on a grassy shelf that afforded a panoramic vista of the surrounding countryside. Nate could see clear back across the plain they had crossed.

Winona and Evelyn strolled to the north end of the shelf. Yellow flowers grew in profusion and Evelyn was bending to pluck one when she called out, "Pa! You should come have a look-see!"

"Not again," Nate said, hurrying over.

The tracks were the oldest yet, a week to ten days, prints made by four shod horses moving uphill in single file toward the same notch they were bound for.

"These mountains sure have gotten crowded since I was

15

away," Ezriah commented sarcastically. "It's getting worse than New York City."

"No place is more crowded than New York," Nate said. The last he'd heard, the population was a staggering two hundred thousand and growing by boatloads of immigrants each year.

"It sure is a puzzlement," Ezriah said, squinting up at the towering peaks. "I reckon the answer is on the other side of this range."

Nate had the same hunch.

They pushed on, alert for signs. Presently Nate thought he spied a couple of riders on an adjoining hill, but they turned out to be a pair of elk grazing at the tree line. Later he spotted white shapes moving high among the rocky crags. Mountain sheep, a dozen or so, gamboling about at dizzying heights no other creature could reach without wings.

Toward the end of the afternoon Nate came to a talus slope. Avoiding the loose rocks and dirt, he angled to the left. Hoof-prints revealed that the four riders had done the same.

Above the talus was the notch, flanked by low cliffs. From the convenient cover of dense firs Nate scoured the immediate area. Only when he was certain it was safe did he venture into the open.

Sparrows flitted overhead. Otherwise there was no sign of life. The Hawken extended, Nate stepped to the gap. More prints were evident, enough to convince him the notch was used regularly by the mysterious riders. He entered the gap dappled by shadow, with his back to the left-hand wall.

Winona imitated him, her rifle to her shoulder. "We could use horses of our own," she mentioned in a tone that hinted it was more than an offhand statement.

"Do you want me to try and steal some if they belong to hostiles?" Nate asked. This would be no worse than what a war party would do to them.

"What is good enough for the Sioux is good enough for us,"

Winona impishly responded. "If the men are white, perhaps they will have a spare mount or two to sell us."

Ezriah overheard her. "Where do you expect to get the money to buy these nags, lady? It won't be with my gold, I'm telling you here and now. I'm not spending a cent until I reach St. Louis. Then I'm going on a spree the likes of which would make John Jacob Astor envious."

As Nate was aware, Astor had made millions in the fur trade and was reputed to be the richest man in America.

"I'll live in a mansion and have servants wait on me hand and foot," Ezriah said. "I'll wear tailor-made clothes that will put the duds I have on to shame. And when I go places, it will be in the most expensive carriage money can buy, one with satin seats and silver trim, pulled by four white horses."

"You have it all thought out," Nate said.

"You bet your britches I do," Ezriah gloated. "I've got a lot of living to make up for. Twenty years' worth. So I'll only eat the best of food, drink the finest liquor, and spend my time in the company of the best-looking women since Cleopatra."

A faint noise from the opening twenty feet away brought Nate to a halt with his arm raised for quiet. A second later a human form was silhouetted against the backdrop of sky. All Nate had was the briefest of glimpses. Then Evelyn hollered, "Pa! Look!" and the figure bolted.

"After him, King!" Ezriah goaded. "If it's an Indian, he'll bring a whole passel down on our heads!"

Nate needed no prodding. He raced out of the notch onto a bluff overlooking a verdant valley but had no time to admire the scenery. Thirty feet below a man clad in homespun clothes was about to enter heavy pines.

"Wait!" Nate hollered.

The man glanced up, his face marked by fear. He had no rifle, no pistols, only a long knife on his left hip.

"We won't hurt—" Nate began, but the fellow dashed into

17

the forest before he could finish. Bounding in pursuit, Nate bawled, "Winona! Keep the others with you!" And then he levered his long legs in a flurry, eager to overtake the man.

Plunging into the undergrowth, Nate paused to listen and was rewarded with the crackle of brush off to his right. Veering in that direction, he caught sight of a patch of checkered shirt. "Come back!" he shouted, but he might as well have saved his breath.

Nate lost sight of his quarry until he burst from the pines to find a massive deadfall ahead, a section of slope where every last tree for hundreds of yards had been toppled, years ago, by an earth slide or chinook. Trunks and branches lay in an impenetrable tangled snarl.

The man in homespun was just disappearing amid the maze. Nate tried one last time. "We mean you no harm!" Again no response was forthcoming, and he hurtled into the tangle, resolved to catch the man no matter what. But it was one thing to want to, and quite another to accomplish the deed with an unending barrier of fallen trees blocking his every step. He vaulted logs. He pushed through branch barriers that tore at his buckskins and scratched at his eyes. He scaled trunks as high as his chest and a few even higher.

Thirty yards in, Nate halted again to listen. Either the man had learned from his previous mistake or he was lying low.

A freshly broken limb gave Nate a clue. Cat-footing forward, he found a heel print, then more broken limbs, all leading him deeper, to a twisted mound of trees stacked the height of his cabin. Reaching overhead, he gripped a limb and pulled himself up.

There were plenty of nooks and recesses, and Nate started to poke into each one. A yell to the north interrupted his search. Winona, Evelyn, and Ezriah were at the edge of the deadfall, Evelyn waving and hopping up and down.

"Pa! Pa! We saw him! He's to the right! The right!"

Nate pivoted. Simultaneously, a latticework of limbs parted and out barreled the man in the checkered shirt. In his right hand was the long knife. Uttering an inarticulate cry, he leaped, shearing the blade at Nate's chest. Instantly Nate swept up the Hawken, deflecting it, and shifted to drive the heavy stock into the man's stomach. But as luck would have it, his foot lost its purchase on a smooth trunk, and the next thing he knew, he was falling.

Somewhere, someone screamed. Nate barely heard. He slammed onto the wide bole with bone-jarring force and the world exploded in a riot of bright dots and dancing colors. Struggling to sit up, he shook his head to clear it.

The man was dropping toward him with the knife upraised to cleave his skull in half.

Nate flipped to one side and the glittering steel thudded into the log instead. Sweeping the Hawken up and around, he clipped his attacker on the back of the legs and toppled him onto his back.

"No!" the man wailed, scrabbling to his hands and knees. "I won't let you! Do you hear me? Not in a million years!"

Nate had no idea what the lunatic was raving about. He gained his feet first and arced the stock at the man's temple to end their clash. But the madman was quicker than he anticipated and rolled out of harm's way.

Reversing his grip, Nate trained the Hawken on the man's abdomen and thumbed back the hammer. At the metallic click, the man froze halfway erect.

"Drop the knife or I'll blow out your wick," Nate warned.

Glaring raw spite, the man reluctantly did as he had been instructed. He was lean of build, with high cheekbones and curly sandy hair. "Do your worst!" he snarled. "I still won't let you!"

"Let me what?" Nate said, utterly mystified.

"As if you don't know!"

David Thompson

"How should I? I don't know you from Adam," Nate stated flatly. "Calm down and tell me what this is all about."

The man's brow creased in confusion. "Are you trying to tell me that he didn't send you?"

"Who are you talking about?" Nate said, inadvertently raising his voice in irritation. "My family and I are passing through on our way home. I saw you—"

"Did you say family?"

"Over yonder," Nate said, and pointed.

Tension drained out of the man like water from a sieve. A lopsided grin curled his mouth and he said, "I'm awfully sorry. There's been a terrible misunderstanding." He began to unfurl, then gazed past Nate and his dark eyes widened in shock. "No! Don't kill him!"

Nate whirled, thinking another man had snuck up on him from the rear. But it was a woman. A petite brunette in a homespun dress who had an ax hoisted aloft, and as he rotated, she swung it at his face.

Chapter Two

Winona King's heart leaped into her throat when she saw the white woman materialize out of nowhere and lift an ax to slay her husband. She snapped her rifle to her shoulder and fixed a hasty bead, but Nate sidestepped the descending ax head, stepping into her sights, and she held her fire. She heard her daughter squeal with joy when Nate grabbed the ax handle and wrenched it from the woman's grasp.

"They didn't hurt him! He's all right!"

"Who are those folks?" Ezriah Hampton wondered aloud.

"Whoever they are, they're sure not very friendly," Evelyn said.

The man in the checkered shirt darted to the woman and they clung to each other, the woman weeping, as Nate ushered them out of the deadfall.

Winona trained her own rifle on the duo, furious at the attempts on Nate's life. Then, as the pair drew nearer and she beheld the misery etching the woman's face, her fury dampened and was replaced by intense curiosity. Up close, Winona

21

saw that their clothes were smeared with grime and the woman's dress had been torn in spots. Both were haggard, with dark splotches under their eyes from lack of sleep.

The woman was in such despair that she tottered when the man let go of her for a moment, and he promptly wrapped his arm around her again to support her.

"Have a seat," Nate directed, nodding at a log. "And keep your hands where I can see them."

Winona's eyes caught his and she smiled, conveying her relief and her love. She kept her rifle on the strangers as Nate tossed the ax aside and planted himself in front of them. The woman's head was bowed and her shoulders were heaving in heavy sobs.

"Now let's find out what this was all about," Nate said. "Start with your names."

The man looked up, anxiety oozing from every pore. "I'm Jack Weaver. This is my wife, Molly."

"I'm Nate King. The woman ready to blow your brains out if you so much as twitch is Winona, my wife. Evelyn, there, is our daughter. And the peacock with the sword is Ezriah Hampton."

"Peacock?" the trapper said.

Nate ignored him. "Why did you run off like you did, Weaver? Why did the two of you try to kill me?"

Jack Weaver gnawed on his lower lip, afraid to reply.

"I'm waiting," Nate said harshly. He felt little sympathy, not after what they had done. They were settlers, was his guess. Both were in their early twenties and undoubtedly green behind the ears, but that was no excuse for their monumental stupidity.

"If we tell you and—" Weaver said, then caught himself. Clamping his lips shut, he shook his head.

"And what?" Nate prodded.

Molly raised her head. Her cheeks were damp and she was

shivering as if she was cold. "Can't you let us be? We're sorry, mister, truly sorry. It was a mistake, is all. We mistook you for an Indian."

"An Indian with a beard?" Nate said skeptically. In all his years in the wild he had only ever met one, and that had been a warrior so hairy he resembled a bear.

"It was your buckskins and your dark hair and all," Molly said. "We thought you were after our scalps and we panicked."

Her excuse didn't quite wash, but for the moment Nate let it pass. "What are the two of you doing here? Do you have a homestead nearby?"

"We're from the settlement," Jack Weaver said.

"Good God!" Ezriah exclaimed. "I was right! It is getting worse than New York City! Why, next thing there will be outhouses behind every tree!"

"Pay him no mind," Nate told the couple. "He was dropped on his noggin when he was a baby and hasn't been right in the head ever since."

Sputtering with indignation, Ezriah rasped, "I was not! And I'll have you know people have always respected me for my pearls of wisdom."

Nate stared out across the broad, lush valley. He saw no evidence of habitation. But intervening trees blocked his view of much of it. "Where's this settlement of yours?"

Jack jerked a thumb to the north. "You can't see it from here. It's called New Eden."

"Never heard of it," Nate said. To a degree, he shared Ezriah's dismay. He had always dreaded that one day pilgrims would swarm to the mountains like bees to pollen, and settlements and towns would spring up everywhere. New Eden might be the beginning of the end for the way of life he enjoyed.

"Colonel Proctor started it up about eighteen months ago," Jack said. "He led a wagon train here for that express purpose."

"Proctor is an army officer?"

"North Carolina militia. He comes from a military family. His grandfather was a famous hero of the Revolution." A certain bitterness crept into the younger man's voice. "The colonel owned a prosperous plantation. He was real rich and powerful. Two terms running he was a senator in the state legislature."

"He gave all that up to start a settlement in the middle of nowhere?" Nate said in disbelief.

"The colonel is a unique man," Jack said.

"Your colonel is a jackass, pup," Ezriah declared. "If I had me a plantation, I'd live out my life in the lap of luxury. I sure as hell wouldn't go traipsing off into the wilds for the thrill of it."

"Oh, Colonel Proctor had a reason," Jack said, but he didn't say what it was.

Molly had stopped crying and was dabbing at her eyes with her sleeve. "Will you please let us go now? Again, we're terribly sorry about the misunderstanding. But we need to be on our way."

"Back to the settlement?" Nate said. "We'll tag along with you."

Both husband and wife blurted "No!" in unison, and Molly leaped to her feet in consternation.

"No, no! We're not going back! Not ever. In fact, we were on our way out of the valley when we bumped into you."

Winona prided herself on being a fair judge of human character, and it was obvious to her the pair were scared to death. Why that should be, she couldn't say. She also sensed they were not being completely honest. "Where were you headed?" she asked.

Jack and Molly visibly hesitated. Finally Jack said, "We're on our way back to the States. We've had enough of frontier life."

Nate did not appreciate being lied to. "Without horses? Without supplies? With just the clothes on your backs and a knife and an ax?"

"It was all we could get our hands on," Jack said.

"But if you intend to return to the States," Winona brought up, "why were you going west instead of east?"

Jack nervously licked his lips. "There are only two ways in and out of the valley. The notch just happened to be closer."

Their story became more preposterous by the moment, Nate mused. "It's good we came along when we did, then. You'd never make it out of the mountains alive." For that matter, they probably needed help crossing a street so they wouldn't be run over by a carriage.

"You're traveling east, aren't you?" Molly said, brightening. "You could take us with you! We'll go up through the notch and around to the south. There has to be another way through this range."

"There is," Nate said, "but cutting across this valley will take a lot less time."

"We're in no rush." Molly clasped her hands to her bosom. "Please, Mr. King. We beseech you. Help us reach Bent's Fort. We'll be fine on our own from there."

"I'd like to see the colonel about buying some horses first."

Again panic gripped them, and Jack said, "He doesn't have any to spare. If he did, we wouldn't be traveling on foot."

"Let's just go, now, while we still can," Molly urged. "Before it gets dark, I mean."

"My wife and I need to talk this over. Stay right where you are," Nate instructed them, and backed off half a dozen yards.

Winona joined him. "What do you think?"

"Something isn't quite right," Nate said.

Ezriah Hampton had tagged along, and he let out with a loud snort. "Hell, anyone with half a brain can see those two are lying through their teeth. If you ask me, they just can't

25

take the strain of living in the wilderness. I've seen it before."

So had Nate. Settlers who tried to make a go of it and failed. The daily struggle for survival, the constant threat of Indian attacks or of being set upon by wild beasts, was more than most could endure. "Maybe, but I suspect there's more to it than that."

"Whatever their problem," Winona said, "the issue for us to decide is whether we will help them. And I think we should. We have come this far without horses, we can go the rest of the way without them."

"Speak for yourself, lady," Ezriah grumbled. "My feet are worn to a frazzle."

"It's those high-heeled boots you're wearing," Nate said. "You should have stuck with moccasins."

"But these boots have such shiny buckles!"

Sighing, Nate walked to the Weavers. "All right. We'll forget about getting horses and help you reach Bent's Fort. But you'll—" He got no further. To his amazement, Jack and Molly threw themselves at him, hugging him close.

"Thank you, thank you, thank you!" Molly said, sniffling. "You don't realize how much this means to us!"

"You've saved our lives!" Jack exclaimed. "And after what we almost did to you! You're a saint, Mr. King! An angel sent to answer our prayers!"

Ezriah Hampton made a show of scrutinizing Nate's head. "I think his halo is on crooked."

Keenly uncomfortable at being held so close by two people who minutes ago had tried to murder him, Nate shrugged free. "As I was about to say, we'll help, but you're to do as I say at all times. Savvy?"

"That's fine by us, yes," Jack said sincerely.

Molly was crying again but now her tears were tears of joy. She gripped her husband's arms. "We've done it! Truly done

26

it! In a couple of months we'll be back in Illinois, safe and sound."

"Illinois?" Nate said. "I thought you were from North Carolina?"

"Oh, no," Molly answered. "The colonel and his people are. We joined up with them when he stopped overnight in the town where we lived."

"We met Proctor at a restaurant," Jack said. "He told us about his grand plan to start a new settlement and we thought it sounded wonderful. So we sold our house and piled our belongings into a wagon."

"Not very bright of us, was it?" Molly said.

"How were you to know what life in the mountains would be like?" Winona responded. "You can not blame yourselves."

Ezriah had to add his two bits. "They could have asked around some first. It's what I did before I headed west. But then, I'm not as dumb as an ox."

"There's more to it than that," Jack said defensively.

"How so?" Winona asked. She very much desired to learn what the twosome were about, but before either could reply, the distinct thud of hooves sounded lower down the slope.

The Weavers staggered as if dealt physical blows. Both became as white as bedsheets, and Molly clutched Jack in terror.

"It's them! They've found us!"

"Who found you?" Nate said.

Shifting, Jack gripped the front of Nate's shirt. "We've got to run! Got to hide! Hurry, before it's too late!"

"Run from who?" Nate tried again. He was tired of their antics. "I want to know what this is all about and I want to know now."

Molly was gazing fearfully down the hill. "It's no use! They're almost here! We tried and we failed. Now all we can do is pray for the best."

Out of the pines trotted three riders, three men in gray

uniforms and caps. Each had a saber about his waist, as well as a flintlock pistol in a covered holster. Each also had a rifle in a saddle scabbard. The lead rider was a lanky, clean-shaven, handsome man with short-cropped brown hair. Chevrons on his sleeves identified him as a sergeant. With a wave of his arm, he led the others upward at a gallop.

"If you have any mercy in your soul," Jack whispered to Nate and Winona, "you won't tell them how we met."

Within seconds the soldiers reined up. The sergeant broke into a broad smile and said good-naturedly, "Well, what have we here? If it isn't Mr. and Mrs. Weaver. And you've made some new friends, I see."

Nate and Winona leveled their rifles. Long ago they had learned the hard way never to take anyone for granted, never to trust a stranger until the stranger proved trustworthy. Nate introduced them, adding, "I have a cabin near Long's Peak. We've had some troubles with hostiles and are on our way home."

"Afoot? That must be rough." Dismounting, the man offered his hand. "Sergeant Michael Braddock, late of the Fourth Regiment, North Carolina Militia, at your service, sir."

Warily, Nate shook. "We just met the Weavers," he mentioned. For a reason even he couldn't fathom, he did as Jack Weaver had requested and refrained from detailing the exact circumstances.

Sergeant Braddock glanced at the pair. "If you don't mind my asking, what are the two of you doing down here? Don't you know how dangerous it can be? We've warned you time and again that until the big parley, we have to be on our guard against raids."

"We just wanted to go for a stroll," Molly said. "It's such a nice day and all, we lost track of the time and how far we had gone."

Jack nodded vigorously. "We were on our way back when we spotted Mr. King and his family."

The old trapper stepped forward. "What about me? Don't I count?" He thrust his hand at the noncom. "Ezriah Hampton. I was in the militia once, in Virginia, about, oh, fifty years ago, give or take a few."

Sergeant Braddock appraised Ezriah from head to toe. "That's some outfit you're wearing, sir. You remind me of a French dandy I met once down to New Orleans. He favored a cloak and coat just like yours."

"He did?" Ezriah said, puffing out his scrawny chest. "Well, those French fellas know how to dress right."

The sergeant turned to Evelyn and gave a courtly bow. "And who is this dazzling young beauty with the fetching green eyes?"

"Oh, my!" Evelyn said, flustered.

Gallantly clasping the tips of her fingers, Braddock lightly pecked them. "It is a rare treat to make the acquaintance of a lovely lady like yourself."

Winona had seldom seen her daughter blush but Evelyn did so now; for the first time in her tender life she was at a complete loss for words.

His brown eyes twinkling, Sergeant Braddock straightened. To Nate he said, "I miss life in the South. Lovely belles with their beguiling manners. Formal balls once a month. Picnics every Sunday."

"Why did you leave if you love it so much?"

Braddock's handsome visage clouded. "I owed it to my commanding officer, Colonel Proctor, to help him form his new militia."

The offhand remark startled Nate. "He's forming a militia *here*? But this isn't the States. It's not even part of any organized territory. This is Indian country. There's no government,

David Thompson

no vested authority." Which was exactly how Nate and every other mountain man preferred it.

"Ah, well. Politics aren't my strong suit, Mr. King. You would have to take that up with the colonel. In fact, if you have no objections, we would be honored to escort you to New Eden so you can meet him."

Jack Weaver coughed. "They're interested in buying horses but we told them there aren't any to spare."

"They might as well be on their way," Molly said.

Braddock seemed to be perplexed. "Speaking for the colonel now, are you? He may be willing to part with a few mounts, for all you know. We certainly have more than enough. There's no harm in asking, is there?"

"No, of course not," Jack said.

Ezriah was rubbing his stomach. "Any chance we could get something to eat at this settlement of yours? I'm half starved."

"I'm sure the colonel will invite you to partake of supper with him this evening," Sergeant Braddock said. "It's meager fare by plantation standards, but the cook does the best he can."

"Cook? The colonel has a cook?" Ezriah showed all his yellow teeth to Nate. "Did you hear that, hoss? Food! Real honest-to-gosh food! How can we pass it up? What do you say?"

Nate balked, and couldn't say why he did. The sergeant was friendly enough and the prospect of obtaining mounts and a decent meal were appealing, but he couldn't forget the raw fear in Jack Weaver's eyes when the man insisted they flee before it was too late. *Too late for what?* he mused.

Evelyn snatched Winona's hand. "Can we, Ma? Please? We haven't visited with people in a coon's age!"

Long ago Winona had learned to master her emotions, never to betray her feelings by her expression unless she wanted to. So now, although she felt apprehensive about tak-

30

ing the soldier up on his offer, she smiled and said, "I would not want to impose on anyone, daughter."

Sergeant Braddock pushed his cap back on his head. "It wouldn't be any imposition at all, ma'am. Colonel Proctor loves to socialize. Back in North Carolina he had supper guests practically every night. Afterward, they'd sit around sipping liquor and talking to all hours of the night."

"Sounds like a gent after my own heart," Ezriah declared. "It would be remiss of us if we didn't pay the man a visit."

"Please, Ma," Evelyn said.

Winona wavered, and as she invariably did on those rare occasions when she couldn't make up her mind, she looked to Nate for his opinion. She trusted his judgment implicitly. Whatever he decided would be fine by her.

Evelyn looked at him, too. "Please, Pa? It will be fun. And we can use the rest, can't we?"

Nate disliked being put upon. But there was no denying they had been through hell and back again, and a little relaxation would do them a lot of good. "I suppose it wouldn't hurt," he said begrudgingly. Out of the corner of his eye he saw Molly Weaver bow her head.

"Then it's settled," Sergeant Braddock said. Stepping to his bay, he forked leather. "Private Yates and I will escort you in while Private Timmons rides to New Eden to inform Colonel Proctor." He gestured at the stockiest of the militiamen, who wheeled his animal and galloped off.

Evelyn was giddy with glee. "I can't wait to meet all the ladies! They can tell us how things are in the States! What everyone is wearing and all!"

Winona experienced a twinge of resentment. Her daughter had made no secret of the fact she intended to live in the States one day, and it upset Winona more than a little to realize Evelyn was more partial to the white way of life than the Shoshone. "Yes, it will be nice," she said.

"If you'll be so kind as to follow me," Sergeant Braddock said, clucking his horse forward.

The Weavers went next, arm in arm, both downcast, acting more as if they were going to their doom instead of returning to where they lived.

Ezriah swaggered in their wake like a cavalier of old, one hand on the hilt of his sword.

Nate and Winona walked shoulder to shoulder, Evelyn skipping along as merry as a lark in front of them. Nate observed that Private Yates waited to go last but didn't think much of it. When soldiers escorted wagon trains they invariably rode flank to protect the civilians.

Winona insured that the soldier following them wasn't close enough to eavesdrop, and whispered, "I am a bit uneasy."

"You too?" Nate said. "Maybe we're making a mountain out of a molehill. The sergeant seems friendly enough. And if they try anything, we still have our guns."

"Why is it we never heard of this settlement? You would think it would be common knowledge."

Nate agreed. Important information traveled fairly fast in the mountains, largely by word of mouth. Campfires took the place of mail service; it was a nightly ritual to share the latest tidings, gossip, and tall tales. A lone trader, making the rounds of the friendly tribes, could relay all the latest news in a couple of months. "Maybe we were gone when word got around."

"But we visited Bent's Fort two moons ago," Winona said. "Surely someone there would have mentioned it."

"You would think so, wouldn't you?" Nate replied.

"Perhaps this colonel wants to keep it a secret," Winona speculated. Although why he would want to was beyond her. Then again, she had learned that whites sometimes did things in defiance of all logic. She still couldn't get over how dependent they were on money, on coins and bills they themselves made. Or how they revered gold as if it were the Great Mystery.

Ezriah Hampton chose that moment to drop back alongside them. "This will be great practice for me."

"You need practice eating?" Winona said with a grin.

"Very funny. No, I need practice getting along with folks. Particularly the fairer gender. I used to be a popular fella with the ladies but I'm not as spry or as witty as I once was."

As the subject of many of his caustic barbs, Winona admitted to him that. "You have no cause to fret. Your mind is as sharp as ever."

"Why, ain't you a daisy!" Ezriah said, tickled. "If I were thirty years younger and you weren't hitched, I'd likely come courting."

"Do you wash dishes?"

"What's that got to do with anything? No, doing dishes is a woman's job, same as doing clothes and planting flowers and such."

Winona feigned a frown. "Then we could never be more than close friends. Nate often helps me wash up after a meal. He helps clean and plant, too."

"He's that sissified? I'd never have guessed, a big, strapping coon like him. It's a crying shame. In my day and age a man would rather walk barefoot across burning coals than be caught doing housework."

A retort was on the tip of Winona's tongue. But just then Sergeant Braddock called out her husband's name and pointed to the north.

"There she is, folks! New Eden!"

Chapter Three

New Eden lived up to its name.

The verdant valley was approximately six miles long and half as wide. High grass ideal for grazing covered the valley floor, sprouting from rich soil ideal for tilling. The adjacent slopes were heavily timbered, providing enough wood to last generations. A gurgling stream flowed from west to east midway along, and a picturesque covered bridge had been erected across it. Beyond the bridge lay the actual settlement.

Nate King was impressed by the orderly manner in which the homesteads had been laid out. Often, new settlements were haphazard affairs, with homesteaders throwing up cabins wherever they liked in a mad scramble for the choicest plots. But the cabins constituting New Eden had all been built in the center of their allotted sections, six on the left of the rutted dirt road, six on the right.

The cabins were twice the size of Nate's own, sturdily constructed and complete with white picket fences and outhouses. In front of several of the homes children were playing. Each family, it turned out, also had a large dog. And all the dogs made a habit out of barking at anyone who passed by.

Sergeant Braddock had fallen back to ride beside Nate and Winona. "The dogs were the colonel's idea," he commented. "To help guard against hostiles."

"They'll help some," Nate said. But as he had learned, watchdogs alone weren't enough. All it took was a single stealthy warrior with a bow to render dogs useless.

The largest dwelling was at the end of the road and belonged to Colonel Proctor. More a log mansion than a cabin, it was two stories high and over a hundred feet long. Glass panes shimmered in every window. Chiseled wooden steps led up to a wide oak door complete with a brass latch and a large brass knocker.

East of the colonel's was a large stable with an attached corral that held seven or eight horses. Smaller outbuildings and several sheds flanked it. To the west of the house was a building bearing a sign in bold black letters: PROCTOR MERCANTILE. In front of it was a hitch rail to which five horses had been tied.

"The colonel has his own store?" Nate marveled.

"He's thinking ahead, as always," Sergeant Braddock said. "One day soon New Eden will boast ten thousand people, maybe more."

"A hundred years from now maybe," Nate replied. He couldn't conceive of anything that would lure that many emigrants to such a remote, isolated spot.

"Oh, a lot sooner than you think, Mr. King," Braddock said, grinning. "The colonel has big plans. Mighty big plans. What he wants, he gets. And he wants New Eden to grow as big as Raleigh in his lifetime."

As Nate recollected, Raleigh was the capital of North Carolina and the largest city in the state. "How does he aim to do it? Pay people to come?"

David Thompson

Braddock chuckled. "He has a better incentive. You'll need to talk to him about it, though. We've all taken vows not to say a word until he's ready for the rest of the world to know."

How strange, Nate thought. But he didn't pry. One of the cardinal unwritten rules of the frontier was that a person's private affairs were just that.

Winona had been studying the settlement with interest, and now she asked a question that begged an answer. "Sergeant, the only people we have seen are children. Where are all the adults?"

"I was wondering the same thing, ma'am," Braddock said. "Maybe they're at a meeting. The colonel calls us all together whenever something important comes up."

From behind the log mansion a burst of excited braying and barking shattered the afternoon. It sounded as if a dozen dogs were in a frenzy.

"What on earth?" Nate said, looking up at the sergeant.

"Those are the colonel's bloodhounds. He has a kennel out back with nine of the finest hunting dogs ever bred. Dotes on them as if they were his kids. It must be feeding time. They always make a racket like that when they're fed."

Ezriah Hampton grinned. "Your colonel likes to hunt coons, does he?"

"He's partial to larger game," Sergeant Braddock said. "Bear, mountain lions, wolves, you name it. Those bloodhounds of his will go after anything."

Just beyond the mercantile were other buildings with wide double doors. One was open, and through it Nate saw a forge and anvil. "You have your own blacksmith shop?"

"Yes, sir. The colonel has thought of everything."

The front door to the mercantile opened and out strode a heavyset man of ruddy complexion with a neatly trimmed red beard. He wore a uniform much like the sergeant's, only his was adorned with gold trim and gold insignia. Ribbons and medals practically covered half his chest, and on his shoulders were large gold epaulettes. Instead of a cap he wore a high-crowned hat, another insignia on the crown.

"That's the colonel," Sergeant Braddock said.

Nate had guessed as much, and the thought crossed his mind that Proctor was more of a peacock than Hampton.

Ezriah was in awe. "That there is some uniform! Maybe I'll get me one just like it when I get back to the States."

Winona was less impressed. The officer reminded her of a certain Nez Perce notorious for strutting around at the annual rendezvous bedecked in pompous finery he acquired in trade. Overwhelmed by his own magnificence, the warrior was unaware he was the laughingstock of the gatherings.

Out spilled more people, men and women, most of the men wearing uniforms, the women in charming homespun dresses.

"I was right. It was a meeting," Sergeant Braddock said. Spurring his bay, he rode up to the porch and briskly saluted. "Sir! While on routine patrol we found the Weavers at the south end of the valley, along with a frontiersman who was passing through with his family and a friend."

Colonel Proctor returned the salute. "At ease, Sergeant. Private Timmons told me you were on your way." Proctor descended the steps and advanced with an outstretched hand toward Nate, a warm smile of greeting creasing his thick jowls. "I assume you have been informed who I am. Welcome to New Eden."

The strength of the officer's grip was mildly surprising. Nate made the introductions, and Proctor shook everyone's hand with equal enthusiasm.

"I can't tell you how wonderful it is to meet all of you. You're our first visitors, as it were, and I hope you will permit me to host a formal dinner in your honor this evening."

Winona had learned enough of white ways to say, "We would not want to put you to any bother."

"My dear woman, it's no bother at all. My servants have little else to do." Proctor had blue eyes that sparkled with vitality. "It will be like the old days in the glorious sovereign state of North Carolina when I entertained almost nightly. How I miss that."

"You're a long way from home," Nate said.

Colonel Proctor surveyed the valley. "New Eden is my home now, Mr. King. It is here I shall live out the remainder of my life. It is here I shall be laid to rest when I go to my reward." He pointed toward a low knoll to the northeast. "There is where they'll bury me."

"You already have your burial site picked?"

"I am a military man, sir. Planning, strategy, tactics, they are my life's passion. I'm always thinking ten steps ahead of everyone else. So yes, I already have my burial site selected. Along with the monument I want erected in my honor, and the inscription that will be engraved on the monument." Proctor paused, then gravely intoned. "Here lies William Harrison Proctor. Visionary, soldier, statesman, and first governor of New Eden."

"Governor?" Nate said, baffled.

The colonel gave a toss of his head and grinned. "Getting ahead of myself again, aren't I? Here. Allow me to introduce you to the others."

The men in uniform had lined up at attention. Private Timmons they had already met. Beside him were Privates Bell, Stewart, Mitchell, Latham, and Danvers. Adding Yates and Sergeant Braddock, that meant eight of the twelve settlers were soldiers, another fact that struck Nate as peculiar.

The other two were Jack Weaver and a burly, muscular man by the name of Carson, whom Proctor described as "our blacksmith, gunsmith, and general wizard of all trades."

All the men were married, and one by one their wives were introduced to Winona, who worried she wouldn't be able to remember all their names. Two of the ladies struck her as being particularly nice: Cecelia Braddock, the wife of Sergeant Braddock, and Agatha Carson, the blacksmith's middle-aged woman.

As Colonel Proctor finished, Winona turned to him and inquired, "What about you, Colonel? You have no wife of your own?"

Proctor became a trifle sad. "Would that I did. But no, alas, I have not yet found my soul mate. Not that I haven't looked, mind you." He clasped his pudgy hands behind his broad back and sighed. "A soldier's lot is not an easy one, Mrs. King. It is similarly hard on a soldier's wife. Perhaps it's for the best I never wed."

"You are still fairly young," Winona said to be polite. She pegged his age between thirty-five and forty. "You might yet meet the woman of your dreams."

"One never knows, does one?" Proctor philosophically replied, then commented, "I must say, your English is impeccable. No trace of an accent whatsoever. My compliments, madam."

Ezriah Hampton had been standing to one side, his hat at a rakish slant, his cloak tossed back over his shoulder, as if posing for a portrait. "She knows a whole bunch of tongues," he piped in. "She's a—what did Nate call her?—a born linguist."

"You don't say?" Colonel Proctor said. "Interesting. Very interesting." Without revealing why he found it so noteworthy, Proctor suddenly pivoted toward the Weavers, both of whom started as if they had been pricked by briars. "Jack and Molly! Don't think I've forgotten about you. How fortunate, is it not, Sergeant Braddock found you when he did?"

"We went for a walk," Molly quickly said. "That was all."

"A rather long walk, wouldn't you say? What were you thinking? Have you forgotten how perilous it is to stray beyond the covered bridge? My men can't be everywhere at once. Until a truce is established, you would be wise to stick close to the settlement. Just this morning Private Bell found evidence of Indians to the north. A small party, plainly spying on us."

"We'll be more careful in the future," Jack Weaver promised.

"See that you are." Proctor placed an arm on the man's shoulder. "Really, Jack. You must learn to listen. It's for your own good. I realize you weren't part of our original group, so perhaps you don't feel bound by the rules I've laid down. But they're for your welfare as much as ours."

"It was stupid of us," Jack said. "It won't happen again."

"See that it doesn't," Colonel Proctor said, smiling, then swiveled toward Molly. "As for you, my dear, it would sadden me beyond measure if any harm were to befall you." He reached out as if to touch her brunette curls, but Molly jerked back.

Nate saw a crimson tingle creep up the officer's thick neck and bloom scarlet in those ruddy cheeks, whether from embarrassment or anger he couldn't rightly say.

Proctor slowly lowered his hand and gazed toward the mansion for several seconds. When he faced around, his composure was fully restored. "So! It's agreed? A formal dinner this evening at, say, seven o'clock? Everyone is invited."

Most of the women began talking excitedly among themselves. The soldiers, still at attention, could only smile.

"As for our four visitors," Colonel Proctor said, "I insist they accept my humble hospitality and lodge in my home for the time being." He held out a palm when Nate went to speak. "Please. I'll brook no dispute. I have plenty of spare rooms in the west wing. My own quarters are in the east wing so you won't disturb me in the least."

"Do you have beds for us to sleep on?" Ezriah asked.

"Of course. Double beds with foot-high mattresses, down pillows, and quilt comforters. You will think you are sleeping on air."

The old trapper lit up like a candle. "You hear that, Nate? Real, honest-to-goodness beds! I haven't slept in one in so long, I've forgotten how it feels!"

Nate saw no harm in accepting the invitation. The officer was friendly enough, and it was only for one night. "We'll take you up on your offer."

"Excellent! Follow me and we'll get you settled in." Colonel Proctor headed toward the log mansion. Almost as an afterthought, he said over a shoulder, "Oh. At ease, men. Sergeant Braddock, would you be so good as to escort the Weavers to their cabin?"

"That's not necessary," Jack Weaver said.

"I insist," the officer responded. After a few steps he gestured expansively at his home. "It's not much compared to the plantation I once owned, Mr. King, but it will suffice until I can have a larger dwelling constructed."

"I'm fixing to have a mansion of my own one day," Ezriah mentioned.

"Do tell?" Colonel Proctor said, smirking. "Well, unless you intend to build it yourself, I suggest you strike it rich. They don't come cheap."

Ezriah wrapped an arm around the leather bag containing his hoard of gold coins. "I'll manage, hoss. And I'll have me a butler, too."

"You'll need more than one servant," Proctor said amiably. "In North Carolina I had a staff of thirty-two. Here I only have five. Even so, each must be clothed and fed and housed, which in itself can become quite costly. To cut overhead, I suggest using slaves. That's what I did at Huntington, my plantation, and I brought the best of the lot with me."

41

Nate's interest perked. "New Eden includes slaves?" It was unheard of.

"Surely you don't expect me to do all the menial labor myself? My father owned slaves, and his father before him. I only regret I had to sell most of mine off when I came West."

Evelyn had been uncommonly quiet, but now she interjected, "I don't think that's right, Colonel Proctor."

"What's that, child?"

"Having people as slaves. No one should ever have the right to own another person."

"I understand your sentiments, my dear. But you're just a little girl. When you grow older, when you acquire a more mature perspective, you will realize slavery is a necessary and worthwhile institution."

A wooden portico framed the entrance. Above it hung a copper plaque etched with the title HUNTINGTON MANOR. As they approached, the oak door opened and a black man in a crisply ironed brown suit and white shirt stepped out and to one side, holding the door open for them.

"This is Thomas. He's in charge of my staff. And the most dependable manservant it has ever been my privilege to own."

"Thank you, sir," Thomas said. He wasn't much over five feet in height. His temples were graying, his hair trimmed short at the back, and there was a suggestion of a mustache under his wide nose.

"Inform the staff we have guests for the evening," Colonel Proctor directed. "Tell Aletha I want clean sheets on their beds and water pitchers and chamber pots in their rooms. Inform Harold supper will be served punctually at seven. I expect him to outdo himself for the occasion."

"Yes, sir," Thomas said.

Reaching the threshold, the colonel turned. "And now, if you will excuse me, my new friends, I have an urgent matter to attend to. Forgive my social lapse, but we will have plenty of time to socialize later." Dipping at the waist, Proctor hustled on down a wide hallway.

Thomas graciously beckoned. "Right this way, if you please. I will show you to your rooms. If I can be of help in any other regard, you have only to ask."

Nate let Winona and Evelyn precede him. The floorboards were polished to a sheen, and on the walls hung paintings and tapestries that once must have adorned the walls of Proctor's plantation.

They came to a spacious room opulent in the extreme. Plush carpet, cushioned mahogany furniture. In a corner by a wide window sat a grand piano, and a long sofa occupied the right-hand wall. Other luxurious touches lent added distinction. On the wall opposite the sofa was an enormous portrait of Colonel Proctor in his uniform with three bloodhounds at his feet.

"This way, if you please," Thomas said, crossing toward a hallway near the portrait.

"Lord have mercy!" Ezriah declared, gaping at a crystal chandelier suspended from the vaulted ceiling. "So this is what it's like to live high on the hog? I can't wait."

Winona was intensely interested in the manservant. He was only the second black man she had ever set eyes on, and she thought she would like to get to know him better.

Half a dozen bedrooms lined both sides. Thomas, halting, announced, "You're welcome to take your pick." Then he looked at Nate. "Will your wife and daughter require separate accommodations or will you share the same one?"

This whole while, Evelyn had been gazing at the manservant as if mesmerized. "How did you know he's my pa? No one told you."

"A lucky guess, little miss," Thomas said, grinning.

"Can I ask you something else, mister?" Evelyn said.

"Anything, little miss."

"Why is your hair like that? All crinkly and curly?"

"I take it you haven't met many blacks in your time."

"Only one. He's a Crow. Stopped by our cabin, but he had a beaver hat on the whole time so I never got to see much of his head."

"A Crow, little miss?"

Nate elaborated. "His name is York. A former slave, I think. He was with the Lewis and Clark expedition, and he liked the mountains so much, he came back to live after the expedition disbanded. He was a trapper for a while. Took a Crow wife, and the tribe adopted him. He's been with them ever since."

"A former slave, you say?" Thomas said, but quietly, as if he did not want to be overheard.

"So I was told. But I've never asked him. Out here a person's past is his own. Maybe you'll meet him one day."

"I would like that very much, sir."

Ezriah opened a door and disappeared inside. A moment later he whooped like a Comanche, and there were a series of loud thumps.

Nate and Winona leaped to the doorway, only to find the white-haired rascal bouncing up and down in abandon on the double bed.

"Look at me! Climb on up and let your hair down!"

"Can we, Ma?" Evelyn asked.

Winona took her daughter's hand and moved down the hall. "We certainly can not. When you are a guest in someone's house or lodge, you must respect their property."

"Why doesn't Mr. Hampton?"

Nate answered for his wife. "Mr. Hampton is an idiot. A likable idiot, but an idiot nonetheless."

Winona walked to the last door on the right to get as far from the trapper's room as possible. The elegant furnishings were nearly identical, including a chest of drawers, a table and chair, and a small mahogany stand next to the bed. They made a circuit, admiring a full-length mirror and a porcelain dog on the dresser.

Evelyn was astounded. "This place sure is fancy."

"Fancier than ours," Nate said from the doorway. But he much preferred their quaint cabin to a home the size of a palace. "How many rooms are there?" he asked Thomas.

"Twenty-seven, sir. Not counting the kitchen or the quarters for the servants, in the back."

"The colonel must be expecting a lot of guests," Nate observed wryly.

"Yes, sir. Once word spreads, he says people will flock here by the thousands," Thomas responded.

"Word of what?"

Thomas acted surprised. "He hasn't told you? My apologies, sir, but I shouldn't say anything more. I imagine he wants to do the honors himself."

At that juncture Evelyn came bubbling out to grasp Nate's fingers and say, "Pa, is it all right if I have this room to myself? Ma and you can take the one across the hall."

"You want to sleep alone?" Nate said, disliking the idea.

"I do at home," Evelyn said. "And it would be fun to have such a great big bed all to myself!"

Winona emerged. She sensed her husband's disapproval and shared it. But to spare her daughter's feelings, she said diplomatically, "We are strangers here, Blue Flower, in a strange house." Blue Flower was Evelyn's Shoshone name. "It is best if you and I share the same room. You will be more at ease, little one."

"But I'm not little anymore!" Evelyn protested. "Why does everyone keep calling me that when I'm a big girl?" She bobbed her chin at the room. "Let me prove it, Ma. Let me sleep by myself and show you I can do it on my own."

Thomas cleared his throat. "If you don't mind my saying

so, ma'am, your daughter will be perfectly safe. No one else is staying here except for Mr. Hampton. All the doors are barred at ten every night, and with those hounds outside no one can get anywhere near the house without us knowing it."

Nate realized the man was only trying to help, but he wished Thomas hadn't said anything. Now Evelyn was more determined than ever.

"Did you hear him, Ma? I'll be safe as can be? Please can I? Please?" Evelyn pumped her mother's arm.

Winona had never been one to give in to unreasonable demands from her children. She was about to say no when it struck her that perhaps *she* was the one being unreasonable. Blue Flower was almost eleven, and by Shoshone standards in five years or so would be old enough to take a husband. Not that Winona would let her daughter marry until Evelyn was at least eighteen. But it might be time to start treating her more maturely. So, against her better judgment, she said, "If your father has no objection, neither do I."

Nate was taken aback. He'd never figured Winona would agree. Now that she had, he was put on the spot. Although his inclination was to decline, he figured Winona must know what she was doing. "If it's all right with your mother, go ahead."

Evelyn squealed in delight and rushed back into the room. Hopping onto the bed, she lay on her back and laughed. "All to myself!"

Thomas opened the door across from hers. "If you folks will excuse me, I must relay Mr. Proctor's instructions to Harold and Aletha."

"Who are they, Thomas?" Winona idly asked.

"Harold is the cook, ma'am. Aletha is one of the maids. She'll be waiting on you while you're here. If you need anything, anything at all, ring for her." Thomas indicated a small bell on the table by their bed.

Nate was reminded of a comment the colonel had made. "There are two other servants, aren't there?"

"Yes, sir. Harriet is Colonel Proctor's personal maid and only attends to him. And then there's Rufus. He mostly works at the stable taking care of the colonel's stallion, and does a lot of odd jobs." Thomas bowed. "I'll return shortly."

Nate watched the manservant hasten away, then entered the room on Winona's heels. "It's a good thing we're only staying one night."

"Why is that?" Winona responded.

"I'm anxious to get home," Nate said. But that wasn't the real reason. He couldn't shake the nagging belief that by agreeing to stay over they had made one of the biggest mistakes of their lives.

Chapter Four

The east wing of Huntington Manor was largely devoted to a spacious dining room worthy of the finest homes on the continent. Three small crystal chandeliers hung at intervals, their sparkling glow playing off the polished oak paneling on the walls. An enormously long mahogany table had been draped with an expensive cotton tablecloth on which sterling silverware had been placed. Crystal glasses brimmed with fresh well water, and neatly folded silk napkins added to the elegance and appeal.

"Quite impressive," Nate King commented as he and his loved ones paused in the wide doorway.

"Thank you," Colonel Proctor said, warmly pumping Nate's big hand. "A man's means should reflect the best his culture has to offer to the fullest extent possible, don't you think? In my modest way I have tried to recreate some of the marvelous atmosphere and setting from my grand days on the plantation."

Again Nate was struck by how much the members of the

colonel's little group missed their old life. "Sounds to me as if you might have been happier staying in North Carolina."

"I was perfectly content there, yes," Proctor conceded. "But circumstances dictated otherwise. So I'm making the best of the situation." He switched his gaze to Winona. "My, you look stunning this evening, Mrs. King."

Winona did not like how his fingers took liberties with her palm but she remained civil and said, "Thank you for having the hot water drawn. My daughter and I enjoyed being able to wash up."

Proctor grinned. "I know how essential baths are to the female constitution. That's another reason I had my Harriet provide scented soap."

Winona looked past the officer at the incredibly attractive young black woman standing to one side. Harriet wore the same smart black-and-yellow uniform Aletha did, but the hem was inches shorter, almost scandalously so, showing her legs clear above the knees, and her ample bosom threatened to spill outward if she were to exhale too hard. Winona thought it a trifle unusual, but she wasn't familiar enough with the customs of the South, in general, and rich whites in particular, to pass judgment. "I thanked her most sincerely."

"It was from my own private stock," Colonel Proctor said.

Winona wondered why a man would have scented soap, then dismissed the thought as unimportant. Easing her hand free of his, she looped it around her husband's arm. "Shall we mingle, my love?"

"Wait for me," Ezriah Hampton said. His clothes had been cleaned by the servants, his square-toed shoes had been polished, and he had even been prevailed upon to wash his face and hands for the occasion. In his mismatched finery taken from the *Sa-gah-lee*, and with the long sword at his waist, he presented quite a sight.

"Mr. Hampton," Proctor said, shaking the oldster's gnarled

hand. "Thomas told me that you liked the cologne I sent."

"Is that what the stuff is called?" Ezriah said. Raising his sleeve to his nose, he sniffed a few times. "It's like a whole field of flowers in one little bottle. I haven't smelled this good since that time I got into my sisters' perfumes."

"I was hoping it would benefit all of us," Proctor said suavely. "You are a walking bouquet."

"You hear that?" Ezriah beamed at the Kings. "Anyone wants to, just walk right up and smell me to your heart's content."

Nate had to admire how cleverly the colonel had hoodwinked the trapper. "I'm more interested in eating than smelling right at the moment," he hedged.

"Supper will be served in half an hour," Colonel Proctor said. "I hope you don't mind it being so late. I wanted you to have the opportunity to mingle and get to know my people before we sat down."

"Thank you," Winona said, making a mental note of how he had referred to the lovely young maid as "his" Harriet, and now to the settlers as "his" people. Evidently he tended to treat everyone just as he treated the slaves; as his personal possessions.

Nate was scanning the room. "I don't see any sign of the Weavers." Which was regrettable. He had wanted to question them about the goings-on earlier.

"They couldn't make it, I'm afraid," Colonel Proctor said. "Something about Molly being out of sorts after their unauthorized gallivant today."

"They needed your permission to go for a walk?" Nate fished for information.

"Certainly not," Proctor answered. "But common sense dictated they at least inform someone. What if something had happened? What if they had run into a war party? We wouldn't have found out until it was too late." Proctor paused.

"I should thank you. Who knows how far they would have wandered if you hadn't come along? You might well have saved their lives."

"It's amazing any of you are still alive," Nate said. "The Blackfoot Confederacy won't take kindly to having a white settlement so close to their territory. Neither will some of the other tribes. Once they learn about it, they're liable to pay your valley an unwelcome visit."

"I've anticipated as much," Proctor said, "and have taken steps to insure we will be allowed to live in peace."

"I remember Sergeant Braddock mentioned a big parley coming up," Nate said.

"One is in the works, yes," the officer admitted. "I'm trying to establish a truce with the neighboring tribes. Perhaps you can advise me in that regard tomorrow or the next day—"

"It will have to be tonight," Nate cut in. "We're anxious to get home. At first light we're heading out."

"Really?" Proctor sounded tremendously disappointed. "Well, we'll discuss it later. In the meantime, my castle is your castle. Mix. Eat. Drink. Make merry. Enjoy New Eden in all her glory."

"You're quite proud of your settlement," Nate said, making small talk.

"Mr. King, you have no idea. New Eden is my brainchild, and mine alone. The settlement might not look like much now, but mark my words, before I'm done, New Eden will rival New York and California for greatness." Proctor was gazing out a benighted window as if into the mists of time. "Did I say rival? No, I meant outshine! In another year or two, New Eden will be the most talked-about subject in the land. Thousands will flock here to join us, and with each new arrival New Eden's strength and prosperity will grow."

"It will take a lot to lure that many people into the heart of the wilderness," Nate remarked.

"I have just the incentive," Colonel Proctor said, but did not say what it was. "Now please, enjoy yourselves. I must check on how Harold is faring in the kitchen. Everything must be just right tonight."

"An intense man," Winona whispered as the Southerner hastened toward a door at the rear, Harriet a second shadow.

"Military men sometimes are," Nate said, although in Proctor's case, he suspected it was more a matter of temperament than training.

Kindly Thomas came toward them bearing a silver tray laden with glasses filled with different liquors. "Would either of you care for a drink?"

Ezriah slid in front of them. "I don't know about them but I sure do! What do you have, hoss? Anything that will rot the enamel right off a fella's teeth?"

"Whatever your desire, sir. Whiskey. Scotch. Rum. The colonel's cellar is well stocked. He has wine for every occasion, as well."

"Wine is for city boys. Real men don't drink bubbly grape juice," Ezriah said. To test a glass, he stuck his finger in and licked it. "Mmm. Mighty fine coffin varnish. How'd he get all this stuff here, anyhow, without busting the bottles?"

"They were packed in flour, sir," Thomas said.

"He must have brought a ton."

"It's a trick emigrants use to keep their eggs and other breakables safe," Nate said. "One family I knew packed all their fine china that way." Abruptly, something dawned on him. "Thomas, where are the wagons that brought you here? I don't recollect seeing any today when we were escorted in."

"The colonel sent them back for more supplies and stock," the manservant responded. "They're not due for another month yet."

Evelyn, Nate noticed, had strayed over to a knot of children and was merrily playing. Nodding to the manservant, he steered Winona toward the far end of the table where the Braddocks and the Carsons were conversing.

"Mr. King, sir," the sergeant said crisply. "A pleasure to see you again. I trust you're finding the colonel's hospitality to be generous?"

"We can't complain," Nate replied.

Cecelia Braddock warmly clasped Winona's hand. "The other ladies and I have been looking forward to getting to know you, Mrs. King. Come, let Agatha and me show you off to everyone."

As the women strayed off, Sergeant Braddock chuckled. "Typical. Our talk was probably boring them silly, Luther."

Luther Carson, the burly blacksmith, nodded. "What do they care about rifles and calibers and whatnot? They'd rather chat about linens and how to cook pot pie. Women are such feeble creatures."

Nate disagreed but he held his tongue. Living with Winona had taught him women were every bit as strong as men. In some respects they were stronger. He would never belittle a female ever again. "You were discussing guns?"

"I believe the colonel told you I'm the gunsmith," Carson said. His upper lip was festooned with a bushy mustache, the ends of which hung down past his jutting jaw. "Mike and I have been debating the best caliber for overall use in these mountains. Perhaps you would care to advise us? We want a real man-stopper for fighting hostiles. I was thinking forty caliber should suffice. Mike says forty-five."

"You'll need to do better than that," Nate said.

"I don't follow."

"Neither are powerful enough. I'll grant you forty caliber is adequate for killing a man, and forty-five caliber a step up. But neither are powerful enough to consistently drop elk and buffalo, to say nothing of grizzlies. I'd recommend fifty caliber or higher. The Hawken I'm using is a fifty-five. So are my pistols." Nate paused. "The same with my wife's weapons."

Carson glanced in surprise toward the woman. "She can handle a gun that powerful? I'd have to see it with my own eyes to believe it."

"Winona is an excellent shot," Nate said. His equal, if not his better.

Sergeant Braddock raised his glass. "My compliments, then, sir. Your lady is one in a million. Cecelia, bless her, couldn't shoot straight to save her sweet soul. She couldn't hit this building if you held the muzzle against it."

Luther Carson roared with mirth.

"She complains a thirty-six caliber is too much," Braddock said. "She doesn't like how gunsmoke stings her eyes, and how black powder gets all over her hands if she isn't careful."

"That's why a woman's place is in the home," Carson declared. "They're too frail for hunting and war."

Into Nate's mind leaped the image of a Crow warrior famed for counting many coup and for bravery in battle. Recently, the warrior had led a war party into Blackfoot country and stolen over seventy horses. In the process, the warrior personally took two scalps. That Crow's name was Woman Chief, and she was as beautiful as she was brave.

"Agatha doesn't agree with me," Carson said. "But she never agrees with half of what I say. Wives are like that," he said, dismissing her opinion. "They always think they know better than their husbands."

"Sometimes they do," Nate had to contribute.

"Once every blue moon," Carson differed. "And we've gotten off the track. I wanted your opinion on how best to arm ourselves, not the foibles of females." He stroked his mustache. "I noticed you tote four pistols in addition to your rifle. Is all that artillery necessary or are you overdoing it a bit?"

Nate briefly detailed his clash with the *Sa-gah-lee*. How his own weapons had been stolen or lost, and he has chosen those he had from the tribe's secret cache. "Normally, two pistols would be enough. But with hundreds of miles to travel—"

"Say no more. I understand," the blacksmith said.

Several soldiers strolled toward them. Privates Latham, Mitchell, and Stewart, the former a shade unsteady from imbibing too much liquor on an empty stomach.

"Mr. King!" Latham said. "The boys and I have been arguing and we're hoping you can set us straight."

"I'll be glad to if I can."

"It's about Injuns," Private Latham said. "Or, to be exact, Injun women. Mitchell, here, claims squaws are as good under the covers as white women. You must have bedded both, and we were wondering how your wife compares—"

Nate punched the militiaman squarely in the mouth.

Latham was slammed back against the table, rattling dishes and silverware and causing all heads to swivel. Latham sagged but didn't go down. His lower lip pulped, blood trickling over his chin, he started to lunge and was met by Nate's fist a second time. Soundlessly, he crumpled, and lay on his back with his eyelids fluttering.

Shock gripped the gathering, but not for long. Stewart and Mitchell and other soldiers angrily advanced.

Sergeant Braddock stepped past Nate to protect him.

It was then the dining room thundered to a roar of outrage. *"What is the meaning of this?"*

Everyone froze. In the rear doorway stood Colonel Proctor, livid with fury, his face as red as blood, his nose flared like a bull buffalo's, his big fists clenched into hams. In the bright light, in his splendid uniform, he appeared like some pagan god of old about to visit celestial wrath on wayward mortals.

"I'm waiting!" Proctor boomed when no one responded. Striding to the table, he stood over Latham, his chest heaving from the emotions he was containing. "Sergeant! Report!"

Braddock snapped to attention. "My apologies, sir. Private

Latham had a little too much to drink. All he did is make a crude comment to Mr. King."

"So crude my guest was compelled to assault him?" Colonel Proctor growled. "What did Latham say?"

"It's nothing," Nate said. "Let it be." He didn't want the festive atmosphere spoiled. Granted, the private had overstepped the bounds of propriety; drunk or sober, some subjects were taboo any time, anywhere. Bringing up intimate details about another man's wife was one of them. It had been a veiled insult, plain and simple, and Nate had upheld Winona's honor. To him that was all that mattered.

Colonel Proctor seemed not to hear. "I'm waiting, Sergeant."

Braddock glanced down at Latham. Reluctance and responsibility waged a private war, and responsibility won. "He referred to Mrs. King as a squaw."

"That's all?"

"Sir?"

"It is a disparaging term, but hardly cause for Mr. King to take violent action. There is more to it, isn't there?"

Nate moved past the noncom. "Can't we drop it, Colonel? I handled it myself. There's no need to involve yourself."

"You're woefully mistaken, sir," Colonel Proctor stated. "As a civilian, you fail to grasp that while New Eden is a settlement, the settlers are military men. These men are militia, under my command. They are subject to rules and regulations, just like soldiers in the U.S. Army. When those rules are broken, it is my responsibility as the commanding officer to insure discipline is swift and just. Now then," he said, glaring at Braddock, "you stand in jeopardy of being insubordinate, Sergeant, unless you quote exactly what Private Latham said to our guest."

When Braddock obeyed, some of the women gasped.

Colonel Proctor became even redder, which Nate didn't

think was possible. The man was a keg of powder about to explode. Yet with remarkable poise, Proctor calmly folded his hands behind his back and announced, "Twenty lashes. Punishment to be administered immediately."

"Lashes?" Nate said.

A collective groan issued from the militiamen, and Sergeant Braddock said quickly, "Begging the colonel's pardon, sir, but isn't that too severe? Ten lashes is standard. Fifteen is more than most men can bear."

"Severe?" Proctor said. "Private Latham slurred a woman's honor. He degraded her in public. Would you have me slap him on the wrist?"

"No, sir," Sergeant Braddock responded. "But twenty lashes—"

"He should consider himself fortunate. Were we in North Carolina, I would add a week in the guardhouse." Proctor faced his men. "Deem me a monster, do you? There's no need to deny it. I can see it in your eyes." Some of the soldiers fidgeted under his withering stare. "I dare any of you to accuse me to my face of being unfair. When you know in your hearts that I have never—never—punished any of you without ample cause."

No one disputed him.

"Private Bell, you earned eight lashes a couple of years ago for sleeping on guard duty. Did you think that was unfair? Given that had it been in time of war, our garrison might have been overrun?"

Bell shook his head.

"Private Danvers, how about you? You received twelve lashes once for being drunk and disorderly. Was that unfair, given that you were going around shooting out lamps and nearly set a home on fire?"

"No, sir, Colonel, sir."

Proctor was relentless. "Now consider this. What if it had

been one of your wives instead of Mr. King's? What if Latham had presumed to ask how your wife is in bed? Would you be so forgiving?"

The silence was thick enough to cut with a butter knife.

"I thought not. Yet you would have me do nothing when our guests have been grievously slurred? Perhaps you think a woman's reputation is only worth five lashes? Or ten?" Proctor's next pause was masterful. "How many lashes are your own wives worth? What meager quota would satisfy your honor?"

Private Timmons stirred. "If someone insulted my wife, sir, I'd whip him down to the spine."

"Same here, sir," Private Yates said.

"Yet all I demand is twenty lashes," Colonel Proctor said. "Yes, it will be painful. But Latham will live. And I can guarantee, gentlemen, that he will never, ever insult another lady as he has done tonight." The officer nudged Latham with a toe. "You will never embarrass me in my own home again, either."

Winona had been a stunned spectator to the sequence of events. Her ears burned, but she was not as offended as the whites made her out to be. She had been to plenty of rendezvous. She knew how white men—and red men, too—became under the influence of alcohol. To her, Latham's remark was a trifle. Her husband had done what needed doing and now it should be forgotten. "Colonel, might I speak in Private Latham's behalf?"

Proctor was astounded. "Madam, do my ears deceive me? You want to defend the man who verbally abused you? I find that most irregular."

"As your guest, and the aggrieved party, I respectfully request that you forgo whipping Private Latham and impose a lesser punishment."

The colonel gave her a look hard to define. "Your grasp of our language, Mrs. King, continues to dazzle me. You are just what I have been looking for." Catching himself, he said, "As for the good private, my men will verify that once I have handed down a punishment, there is no canceling it. No lessening its severity. My judgment is law, Mrs. King. My orders are inviolate."

"A wise leader knows when to be lenient," Winona tried again. "This is a special occasion in our honor, is it not? Surely, then, it is proper for me to request that you reduce the punishment? As a personal favor to one of the guests of honor?"

Colonel Proctor's features clouded and for the longest while he was as still as a stone statue. "You have put me on the spot, madam," he said at last. "On the one hand, military protocol demands I abide by my decision. On the other, social convention requires I give your request serious consideration."

"Twenty lashes is much too many," Winona said. "Two would be more than enough."

"For a minor infraction, yes. In this case, the severity merits more." Proctor nudged Latham again and the private revived just in time to hear the officer declare, "Ten lashes. Sergeant Braddock, you will personally administer the whip. All personnel under my command are required to attend."

Sergeant Braddock pointed. "Private Timmons, Private Danvers, you will take Private Latham to the post."

Nate turned to the blacksmith. "The post?"

"The whipping post. It's out behind Huntington Manor," Luther Carson revealed. "The colonel had it put up the day after we arrived. He had another just like it on his plantation. Used it to keep his slaves in line."

"He whipped his slaves?"

"Only when they deserved it. When they got too lazy for their own good or tried to cause trouble, or ran off. Runaways have become more and more of a problem of late, what with all that damn Yankee talk about how slavery is evil and should be abolished. The simpletons!"

Timmons and Danvers had seized Private Latham by the arms and hauled him to his feet. Latham was bewildered and offered no resistance as they propelled him to the hall and bore to the left.

Winona tried a final time, a direct appeal to the commanding officer. As the colonel walked by, she made bold to place a hand on his arm. "Please forgive my rudeness and reconsider."

"Your persistence is commendable," Colonel Proctor said, "but now it borders on nuisance. I would never presume to tell the Shoshones how to live; kindly refrain from telling me how to conduct military affairs."

The women were abuzz as their husbands tramped out, leaving only the blacksmith, his wife, and the servants. Winona was tempted to press the issue but knew it would only aggravate Proctor. Going to Nate, she said softly, "Maybe you can succeed where I couldn't. Talk to him for me, man to man. Convince him not to go through with it."

"You're asking the impossible, but for your sake I'll try." Nate hurried out after them and saw the last of the troopers turn into another hallway farther down. When he reached the junction they were at the end of a short corridor, filing out into the night.

Nate fell into step behind them. Once outdoors, they slanted toward the kennel, a shoulder-high fence that surrounded nine separate doghouses, each with an individual run. The bloodhounds had their big noses pressed to the fence and were observing the proceedings with interest.

Colonel Proctor halted ten feet from a thick pole imbedded in the ground. He barely acknowledged Nate's presence when Nate tapped him.

"My wife asked me to try one more time."

"Mr. King, I admire your woman immensely. But not even the Almighty himself could stop me from dispensing justice." Proctor thrust an arm overhead. "Sergeant Braddock! Prepare to administer the bullwhip!"

Chapter Five

Nate King need not have stayed to witness the whipping. But, like Winona, he felt indirectly responsible for the private's punishment and elected to remain out of a nagging sense of guilt. He had never meant for anything like this to happen. Knocking Latham to the floor should have ended it. He never realized Colonel Proctor would intervene or impose such harsh discipline.

The militiamen lined up in a grim row facing the pole. A rope was procured, and Private Latham was bound to the upright after first being instructed to remove his shirt.

Private Bell was sent back into the mansion. When he returned, he carried a coiled bullwhip, which he handed to his immediate superior.

Frowning, Sergeant Braddock uncoiled the whip and flicked it a few times hard enough to make loud *cracks*. He stepped to one side of the pole and solemnly regarded the accused, his heart clearly not in what he was about to do.

To Nate's considerable surprise, Private Latham offered no

protest. The man didn't object or plead for leniency or try to break loose. He simply slumped against the broad pole, resigned to his fate.

Light spilling from a rear window bathed the scene as Colonel Proctor stepped closer to the accused. Beyond him eighteen feral eyes glittered like burning coals as the bloodhounds looked on.

Proctor drew himself up to his full height. "Have you anything to say for yourself, Private, before punishment is rendered?"

"No, sir," Latham said contritely.

"I take no pleasure in this," the colonel declared. "But I insist on maintaining proper military decorum at all times. Off duty as well as on duty. You know that. You know my men are required to be on their best behavior at social functions. Your lapse was a serious breech of my trust in you, Latham."

"I'm sorry, sir."

Nate was flabbergasted. Latham was about to be on the receiving end of a severe whipping, and *he* was the one apologizing to the man who had, in Nate's opinion, wrongfully ordered it. In a flash of insight Nate saw that the North Carolinians were extraordinarily devoted to their commanding officer, so much so that they would let themselves be beaten for trifling infractions.

"Prepare yourself, Private," Colonel Proctor said, and nodded at Sergeant Braddock. "On my count. One!"

The bullwhip sizzled in the cool night air, the lash biting into the soldier's back above the shoulder blades. At the *smack* of leather on flesh, Latham stiffened, his mouth wide, but he uttered no sound. Simultaneously, the bloodhounds let out with bloodcurdling howls that wavered on the wind like the cries of spectral demons.

"Two!"

Again Braddock's arm arced, again the bullwhip streaked

true, again Private Latham stiffened, and again the blood-hounds brayed in beastly chorus. A dark stain blossomed on Latham's upper back, dark ribbons spreading downward as the blood flowed toward his waist.

"Three!"

And so it went, the lash slicing again and again into the private. While Nate had witnessed far worse atrocities, none, in his estimation, had ever been so unnecessary. He developed a strong resentment toward Proctor and a begrudging respect for how stoically Latham held up.

Along about the seventh stroke, though, the private's knees gave way and he sagged against the sturdy post, gasping and groaning. The next descent of the lash provoked a low outcry, which Latham stifled by clamping his teeth together.

In the hands of an expert, a bullwhip could cut a man to ribbons. Nate fully expected Latham to be a bloody ruin by the tenth blow. But except for cuts high on his shoulders, he was largely unhurt. The blood made it appear worse than it actually was. And Nate divined why.

Sergeant Braddock was deliberately striving to spare Latham as much hurt as possible. Instead of striking low on the back where the whip would do more damage, Braddock was landing the blows on Latham's well-muscled shoulders so they absorbed most of the punishment.

It gave Nate an inkling of how much Braddock must care for the men under him, and the lengths the noncom would go to in order to help them.

The count was on ten when Nate glanced to the west at the full moon and happened to catch sight of a pale face at the far corner of Huntington Manor. It was there, and it was gone, but he was sure his imagination had not been playing tricks on him. And he was positive it had been Jack Weaver. He did not let on, though, and in another few moments Latham's ordeal concluded.

Sergeant Braddock immediately barked at Timmons and Danvers, who untied Private Latham and bore him into the manor. The rest had to wait to be dismissed by the colonel, who had a few comments to share.

"As distasteful as this was, let it be an object lesson for all of you. New Eden is being founded on the loftiest of ideals and purest of principles. We have not traveled across half a continent and toiled so hard merely to perpetuate the mistakes of the society we have forsaken. New Eden will be a shining beacon, an example of humankind at its best, not its worst."

The militiamen were hanging on his every word.

"Never forget. In the new order to arise, all of you will hold prominent positions. You will be men of influence, men of power. And as such, it behooves you to set an example for all those who will come after us. To live as we would have them live. To show, by your excellence, that they, too, can aspire to perfection."

Nate had a feeling there was more to what Proctor was saying than was apparent, that it had to do with more than the militia.

"The wilderness is about to give birth!" the colonel crowed. "In a day or two the flag will be done! A parley with the Indians is being arranged even as we speak! It won't be long before all the pieces are in place and New Eden will arise to claim her rightful heritage and leave an enduring legacy for posterity."

The vague unease that had plagued Nate since he arrived at the settlement took on form and substance. The North Carolinians were up to something, of that there could be no doubt. Since it involved a flag, it was political in nature, and politics always spelled trouble. If he could, he'd whisk his wife and daughter out of there that very second. But they wouldn't get far at night without horses. So he deemed it prudent to wait until morning and part on friendly terms.

Proctor was striding toward him. "I'm sorry you stayed to observe that, Mr. King. Let's put it behind us. Come back inside and we will turn our attention to much more pleasant matters."

The women and children were seated at the long table, patiently passing the time. Winona and Evelyn had been placed on Nate's left, Ezriah on his right, near the head of the room.

"About time you fellas got back," the old trapper groused. "I'm so hungry, I could eat an elk raw."

A glass of whiskey had been poured for Nate, courtesy of Winona, and he gratefully downed a mouthful that seared his throat and warmed his stomach.

Winona was sensitive to her husband's mood and thoughts, and she perceived he was deeply troubled. Leaning toward him, she whispered, "What is it?"

"Later," Nate whispered. When no prying ears were near to overhear.

The soldiers were filing into the room. Colonel Proctor moved to the head of the table and Thomas pulled out the chair so he could sit. Thomas also brought a glass on a silver tray. The colonel polished off the drink in a couple of quick gulps, then raised his arms for quiet. "Friends! Let us forget the tawdry incident of the last hour and devote ourselves to fine food and merriment!"

"And liquor!" Ezriah called out.

Laughter rippled as Colonel Proctor sat down. He clapped his hands, and at the signal the door at the rear opened and in bustled Aletha and Harriet bearing large trays laden with food.

Behind them were two blacks Nate hadn't yet met. One was tall and lean, in his mid to late forties, and wore a white chef's hat. Harold, the cook, Nate guessed. The other was big and beefy and appeared uncomfortable in the brown servant's uniform he had on. It had to be Rufus, the stable hand, who evidently was required to work at the manor on special occasions.

"Ah, Harold!" Colonel Proctor declared. "I trust you've outdone yourself as I requested?"

The cook brought a special tray and set it before the lord of the manor. Proctor took one look and smiled broadly. "This is a sample? I do believe you've done it! Ladies and gentlemen, prepare to have your taste buds tantalized!"

It was no exaggeration. Tray after heaping tray was placed on the table, filling it from end to end with enough food to feed a literal army. Succulent roast venison, soft-boiled venison, and thick, juicy slabs of elk meat cooked to a turn were enough to set Nate's mouth to watering. Bear meat had been prepared, garnished with wild onions. For added variety, squirrel meat and opossum were presented, the former roasted in thin strips, the latter in a thick, gooey stew that the Southerners were particularly fond of.

Nate had not seen a chicken coop anywhere in the settlement but there had to be one. Fresh eggs were arrayed; scrambled eggs, poached eggs, fried eggs, eggs and bacon, eggs and flapjacks.

A delicious ham was served, a rarity on the frontier, and the meat Nate partook of first. Forking a piece into his mouth, he closed his eyes and savored the exquisite salty, tangy flavor.

Breads, rolls, and biscuits were everywhere. Jellies and jams were ready at hand. Three kinds of soups were on hand for those who were so inclined. Thick butter made the rounds. All in all, it was a feast the likes of which Nate had seldom indulged in, and for a while he forgot about Latham, forgot about his misgivings, forgot about Colonel Proctor and New Eden. He ate, and ate, and ate some more, adrift in bliss. Nor was he alone.

Ezriah Hampton continually chortled with glee as he stuffed

one food after another into his mouth and chomped like a ravenous bear fresh out of hibernation. For a man his size, he ate a prodigious amount, filling himself "to the ears" as he described it. And in some unusual combinations. He dipped a slab of elk meat in his stew. He layered his venison with jam. He took a large chunk of bread, broke it in half, placed eggs and bacon between the halves, and ate the whole thing in gigantic bites.

Winona limited herself to a modest meal. She was hungry enough to eat a lot more, but too much food had a tendency to make her sluggish and sleepy and she wanted her wits about her for the remainder of their stay. She distrusted Proctor immensely, and was keenly worried what he would do when the meal was over.

Winona had a secret, important information she had learned while Nate and the men were outside, information she dearly desired to share with her man. But Proctor was on her immediate left, so close she could reach over and touch him if she were so inclined, and she dared not try with him so near.

Lucille Timmons was the one who had let the information slip. Winona had gone to the window to see if she could spot Nate and the others, and Lucille had come right over.

"Now, now, dearie, don't bother yourself over the menfolk. They'll be back soon enough." Lucille was a big-boned woman with auburn hair done up in a bun. "It's a pity you had to be a party to this your first night here, but Clive Latham never could hold his liquor."

"I'm sorry it happened," Winona said.

"It's done. Over with. Forget it. The rest of us have."

"You're not upset Colonel Proctor is going to have Latham whipped?" Winona inquired. None of the other women appeared to be, either, including Latham's own wife, who at that exact moment was joking and laughing with several of the ladies.

"Whatever for?" Lucille responded. "We're used to it, dearie. To a soldier's life, I mean. Now, if they were going to hang him for desertion, then it would be different. But a few strokes of the lash aren't anything to lose sleep over."

"Ten strokes," Winona said.

"Oh. So that's what has you in a dither? Relax. Mike Braddock can flick a fly off your shoulder at fifteen paces and not break the skin. He knows what he's doing. He'll make it look good, but Latham won't be all that hurt. Just real sore for a couple of weeks, until he mends."

"I still don't see how you stand it," Winona said, referring to the lot of being a trooper's woman.

Lucille Timmons misconstrued. "New Eden isn't that awful. We have nice homes, good land, game is abundant, and water is a short walk away. And in a couple of years, when the city sprouts, we'll be able to stroll down the boulevards and shop to our heart's content." Lucille gave Winona's arm a friendly squeeze. "You'll see. You'll like it here immensely."

"We're leaving in the morning," Winona said.

"You are? That's not what I heard. The colonel doesn't want you to go. And when the colonel wants something, he generally gets his way."

Winona was sure she misunderstood. "Colonel Proctor can't keep us here against our will."

"You have a lot to learn, Mrs. King. The colonel can do pretty near anything he desires. That is why he's the colonel." Lucille clapped her hands together and smiled angelically. "He's so dashing in that uniform of his, don't you think? So strong and virile! He'll make a marvelous governor."

"He's going to appoint himself governor of New Eden?"

"Oh, no, silly goose!" Lucille laughed. "We'll vote him into office. Once he's worked out the details with the neighboring tribes and has them under his thumb, our dream will begin to come true. We should hear back from the half-breed he hired any day now."

So much was being thrown at Winona so fast, she was bewildered. "Colonel Proctor hired a half blood to contact some of the other tribes?"

"Why, you're just a bundle of questions, aren't you?" Lucille responded. "Yes, indeed. The breed is part Crow. We met him on the prairie, and he knew enough English to get by. So the colonel made him a proposition." She tittered. "He's been sent to the Crows, the Flatheads, the Piegans, the Bloods, and some others whose names escape me, to set up a peace parley."

Winona was horrified at the news. The Piegans and the Bloods were part of the Blackfoot Confederacy, who hated whites with a hatred bordering on obsession. They would no more sit down to talk peace than they would take up knitting. The breed was a fool to go into their country alone, and Proctor was a bigger fool to send him.

At that second some of the women had called to Lucille, and she had traipsed off after giving Winona another friendly squeeze.

Now Winona sat at the table yearning to confide in her mate but unable to because Colonel Proctor was bound to overhear, and she didn't want Proctor to know she had an inkling of what he was up to. If all went well, they would retire to their room afterward, arise before the crack of dawn, and slip out of New Eden with no one the wiser. That was Winona's plan, anyway.

At the conclusion of the meal the trays were swept away by the servants, and Colonel Proctor rose. Instantly everyone fell silent and all eyes were trained on their leader. "Before Harold has dessert brought out, a few words are in order. First, let us heartily, and formally, welcome the Kings to our humble settlement."

Glasses were raised and clinked together at the toast.

Ezriah Hampton, gnawing on a piece of buttered biscuit, stopped chewing long enough to grumble, "Why didn't he mention me? Half the time these people act as if I don't exist." He ran a hand along his cloak. "And me in my best duds, too. It's downright humiliating."

Colonel Proctor wasn't done. "Good people of New Eden, in a day or so Lame Bear is due to return. With him rides our hopes. I have every confidence our offer will be accepted by all parties involved, and before the year is out we can send an emissary to Washington."

Cheers rose to the rafters.

Nate was mystified as to how the nation's capital fit into their scheme. His expression must have betrayed his confusion because the officer looked directly at him and chuckled.

"I can tell one of our guests is in need of enlightenment, so perhaps it's time we laid our cards on the table, so to speak." Proctor glanced toward the kitchen door, where Thomas stood. "Inform Harold dessert will be delayed a few minutes."

"As you wish, sir."

The colonel did as was his custom and clasped his hands behind his back. "Now then, where to start? Conventional wisdom has it the beginning is best, and in our case it began in North Carolina about three years ago when I was passed over for promotion. Me, if you can believe it! My record was impeccable, yet the review board saw fit to bestow the honor on an associate of mine who couldn't polish his own boots without help."

Some of the men and women laughed.

"It was my first intimation that my career might be tarnished by factors over which I had no control," Colonel Proctor said. "Instead of one day rising to the rank of general, I foresaw myself languishing for a lack of confidence by those who, on paper at least, were my betters." He paused. "It was totally unacceptable."

Nate couldn't see what any of that had to do with New Eden but he kept his reservations to himself and let the man go on.

"I have always known I was destined for greatness, Mr. King. I have always felt the hand of the Almighty on my shoulder, guiding me. I had always assumed I would distinguish myself in a military capacity, but when my promotion was rejected my eyes were opened and I saw that to succeed, to become the man I'd always envisioned myself being, I had to take certain bold steps. I had to take my destiny into my own hands and create my own path to greatness."

Ezriah snorted and slapped the table. "Ain't he got a pretty way with words? I swear, I could listen to him spew hot air until the cows come home."

Colonel Proctor's lips twitched. "If you please, Mr. Hampton, kindly refrain from glib comments until I'm done."

"Is that what they are? Glib?" Ezriah snickered. "And here I thought it was plain old English."

Nate had to admit he was curious to learn more. He still failed to see the link between North Carolina and New Eden, and said as much.

"Bear with me a little longer," Proctor said. "You see, as I studied the situation, I became more and more convinced that in order to rise to the heights of prominence, I had to cut away from the herd, as it were. I had to make a clean break from the status quo. And what better place to start anew than on the frontier?"

The idea wasn't all that far-fetched. Nate knew of many men who had come West and reaped fame or fortune or both. Jim Bridger, Kit Carson, John C. Fremont, Joseph Walker, Jed Smith—he could name a dozen or better, easily.

"So I pondered my options long and hard, my friend," Proctor said. "I considered entering the regular army, but favoritism is as rife there as in the state militias. I considered a career in politics, but only Oregon and California are organized enough to make a political career practical, and competition for important seats is too fierce to guarantee success."

Nate began to discern where the talk was leading. "So you decided to go everyone one better."

"Precisely. Since I couldn't find a state to suit my purpose, I decided on another course of action." Proctor's face lit with a strange glow. "It was a true revelation! Why settle for clawing out a niche in an already established state when I could carve out an entire state of my own?" He looked expectantly at Nate. "What do you think of the idea?"

"It's"—Nate chose his response with care—"unusual. Last I heard, the United States government lays claim to almost all land between the Mississippi River and the Pacific Ocean. That includes the Rockies." Just a few years previous, the Republic of Texas had been annexed into the United States, and more recently the United States and Britain had finally settled the forty-ninth parallel issue. Now there was talk of buying the Southwest from Mexico, or, as some advocated, annexing it by force of arms.

"A mere technicality," Colonel Proctor went on. "The truth is, our country has outgrown the ability of our politicians to govern it. They have no idea what to do with all the land west of the Mississippi. Some call it the Great American Desert and want to sell it to France or England. Others say we should leave it for the Indians and maintain it as a giant hunting preserve. Hardly anyone wants to live here."

"True," Nate acknowledged. Which was fine by him.

"So imagine how receptive Congress will be to the idea of a group of dedicated men and women carving a new state out of whole cloth? We propose to send an emissary to Washington to outline our plan to create the state of New Eden. Oh, at first they'll probably want us to organize as a territory. But our eventual goal is full statehood."

"With you as the very first governor?"

"What's wrong with that? New Eden is a product of my genius. It's only fair. And all the fine people you see here"—Colonel Proctor included everyone present with a sweep of his arm—"will be rewarded for their faith in me by becoming civic and financial pillars of the community."

Sergeant Braddock, directly across from Nate and Winona, nodded. "We'll each be given five hundred square miles of land to portion out as we see fit. Once people start flocking here from the East, we'll all be rich."

"*If* people flock here," Nate amended.

"They will," Colonel Proctor said confidently. "Once they hear how cheap the land will be compared to land east of the Mississippi, they'll come in droves. Within two years we'll have a fair-sized city. Within five years, a population big enough to apply for statehood."

"You have it all worked out."

Winona had been quiet long enough. "You have not heard all of it, husband. He has not told you about Lame Bear."

"Who?" Nate said.

Colonel Proctor answered. "No one of consequence. A breed I hired to ride to the outlying tribes and invite them to parley. I propose to offer them trade goods in exchange for their promise not to raid New Eden."

Nate sat up, the full import of the officer's blunder knifing into him like a sword blade. "Which tribes?"

"What? Oh, the Crows, for starters. Then I told Lame Bear to go to the Flatheads, the Nez Perce, the Piegans, the Bloods—"

"You didn't."

"What's wrong? It's a simple precaution to insure against future attacks, and buy us crucial time. The Indians will leave us alone until we're strong enough to stand up to them with an army of our own."

Nate surveyed the table and realized none of the others realized what they were in for. "My advice to you is to pack up now, while you can, and get out of here."

"Leave?" Proctor scoffed. "After all the time and effort we've invested? Why would we be so blatantly stupid?"

"Because what you've done is commit suicide," Nate said. "Sending a messenger to the Blackfoot Confederacy is the worst mistake you could have made."

"Surely you exaggerate."

"Let me rephrase it," Nate said in order to make his point. "If you don't leave as soon as you can, by the end of the month there won't be a man, woman, or child left alive in New Eden."

Chapter Six

"Why do we have to whisper, Pa?"

Nate, Winona, and Evelyn King were huddled in the dark in their daughter's room, by her bed. The evening's socializing had ended half an hour ago, and Nate and Winona had come to a decision. "We don't want anyone to know we're getting set to leave," Nate informed his youngest.

"In the morning, you mean?"

"No. In about an hour," Nate said. Time enough for the militiamen and their families to return to their cabins and turn in. Time enough, too, for everyone else at the mansion to drift into dreamland.

"So I get to stay up even later?" Evelyn said, her teeth white in the gloom. "That's fine by me."

Winona never could understand why her pride and joy took such immense delight in staying up as late as possible. When she herself was a child, she had always gone to bed early, and never minded. Then, too, it had never occurred to her to ask to stay up later. Shoshone children generally did as their parents wanted with no argument, whereas many white children, she had learned, badgered their parents to distraction to get their own way.

"What about Mr. Hampton?" Evelyn asked. "We're not leaving him behind, are we? I like him."

"No, he'll go with us," Nate said. But he wouldn't let Ezriah know until the last minute. The cantankerous trapper might not be as eager to go, and was apt to raise a fuss. "We'll wake him when it's time." From down the hall rumbled Ezriah's snores.

"That leaves the Weavers, husband," Winona said.

"You want to take them, too?"

"You saw them today," Winona said. "You saw how scared they are. They were not out for a walk. They are so desperate to leave New Eden, they were willing to run off with just the clothes on their backs."

Nate mulled over how best to proceed. They could stop at the Weaver homestead on their way out of the valley, but that would delay them, and once they were on the go he didn't want to stop for hell or high water. It was imperative they put as much distance behind them as they could, fast, in case their escape was discovered. "I'll slip out and let the Weavers know. It will give them time to pack a few things and be ready when we are."

"Do you know which cabin is theirs?" Winona inquired. No one had mentioned it to her.

"I think so." Nate remembered Jack and Molly sadly gazing at the third cabin to the west of the road as they went by.

Evelyn put her hand on his. "Be careful, Pa. It's going to be hard to be sneaky with all those dogs around."

Nate had been thinking the same thing. But he had it to do. He pecked her, then hugged Winona. "I'll leave my rifle with you. Stay together until I get back. It shouldn't take me more than half an hour."

"Are we leaving because of the Indians?" Evelyn asked.

"We're going to save these people in spite of themselves," Nate whispered. "We'll go straight to Bent's Fort and let Ceran St. Vrain know what they're up to. If anyone can talk them into leaving before the Blackfoot Confederacy wipes them out, he's the one." An honorable, honest man, St. Vrain had partnered up with the Bent brothers to build Bent's Fort, the premier trading post in that neck of the country. Everyone, whites and red men alike, respected St. Vrain highly. His experience was vast, his judgment seasoned by wisdom, his word his bond. And he could talk rings around a tree.

Nate quietly stepped to the door, listened a moment, and cracked it open. The darkened hallway was deserted. With a little wave to his loved ones, he eased out and shut the door behind him, then entered the bedroom across the hall. Parting the curtains, he gripped the sash bar on the window and tried to raise it, only to find the window wouldn't budge. Running his fingers over the bottom rail, he discovered why. *The window was nailed shut.*

Thwarted, Nate went back out and hastened down the hall to the lavish parlor. The manor was as still as a tomb but he couldn't shake a nagging conviction he wasn't the only one up.

Turning right, Nate glided to the entranceway. The door had been bolted but the bolt was well oiled and moved freely without noise. The same with the latch. He opened the door an inch and peered out.

New Eden lay in tranquil repose, bathed in the pale glow of the magnificent full moon. Somewhere a dog barked. Off in the forest a coyote answered with a strident series of yips.

Nate slid out, carefully shut the door, and crept down the steps. A glance confirmed no windows were lit, but to be safe he hugged the base of the wall until he was almost to the corner. As he was about to dart toward the road, the pad of footsteps and the sound of heavy breathing brought him up short. Flattening, he tensed as shapes materialized out of the night.

Coming around the side of the manor was a militiaman with a bloodhound on a leash. The dog had its nose to the ground and was sniffing loudly. The man was Private Bell, and as Nate looked on, he yawned in boredom and gave an angry tug.

"Quit pulling so hard, you mangy mutt. Who do you reckon you're fooling? You don't smell anything except that bitch in heat Mitchell owns."

As if to prove him right, the bloodhound gazed toward the cabins and uttered a low whine.

"Hell, dogs aren't no different than people," Bell said. "All they ever have on their mind is one thing."

Only yards from Nate, the pair halted. The bloodhound lifted its muzzle and gave another loud sniff.

"Cut that out. It's annoying me."

Nate saw the dog look in his direction and he bunched his leg muscles to spring. But the bloodhound never barked or otherwise let on he was there. While its sense of smell was second to none, its eyesight was no better than any other dog's. And in the pitch-black shadow of the manor, he was invisible.

Private Bell switched his rifle from his left arm to his right and the leash from his right hand to his left. "Damn newcomers," he muttered. "I could be home cuddling with my missus along about now, but the colonel doesn't want his guests skipping out on him. So I'm stuck until dawn."

The bloodhound stared toward the cabins and whined again.

"Keep that up and I'll kick you where it will hurt the most." Yanking on the leash, Bell resumed his patrol, making a circuit of Huntington Manor.

Nate waited until they were out of sight, then rose in a crouch and cat-footed to the road. The moon was both a blessing and a curse. A blessing, in that it lit up the valley well enough for him to spot men or dogs a long way off. A curse, in that it was a double-edged sword, and they could just as soon spot him.

Staying tucked low at the waist, Nate jogged past the foremost homesteads. The cabins were set far enough back that with any luck, the watchdogs wouldn't hear him or catch his scent.

In the mountains to the west a mountain lion screamed, a hair-raising cry that could unnerve those unaccustomed to it. The scream set a dog to the south to howling its fool head off, which, in turn, set some of the other watchdogs to joining in.

Nate didn't mind. The settlers were undoubtedly used to the ruckus their dogs made at night, and would only awaken if the dogs started barking. Soon he passed the next pair of homesteads. He moved faster, anxious to return to Winona and Evelyn, but he hadn't gone more than another ten yards when movement ahead compelled him to throw himself to the side of the road on his belly.

Something was coming toward him.

Nate's hands swooped to his waist and he gripped two of his four flintlocks. He would avoid bloodshed if he could, but he wasn't going to let anyone stand in his way. His family was leaving New Eden, and that was that.

The movement coalesced into several four-legged creatures walking down the middle of the road. Two does and a buck, their ears pricked, poised to bolt at the slightest hint of danger. When a dog to the east commenced yowling at the moon, they froze, testing the breeze until assured it was safe to continue.

Nate stayed put, reluctant to spook them for fear they would

80

go bounding off and incite all the dogs within earshot into a frenzy. The trio were twenty feet out when the buck detected his presence. Snorting, it wheeled and pranced off the way they had come, the does flanking it.

Too much time was being lost. Pushing up off the ground, Nate ran to the picket fence that surrounded the third cabin. He looked and looked but didn't see a guard dog. Encouraged, he stalked along the fence to the rear, then gripped the top and vaulted over. No growls or yips greeted him, and within moments he gained the rear wall. He had hoped there would be a back door but there wasn't.

Working his way around to the front, Nate came to a side window. He tested it, and the bottom rail rose high enough to admit him. Amazed at their oversight, Nate hiked a leg over the sill and slowly slipped inside. As his eyes adjusted, he saw he was in a bedroom. A couple of dark forms occupied a double bed to his left. Neither was snoring, but judging by their breathing, they were deep in slumber.

In order to avoid scaring them half out of their wits, Nate moved toward the bed to quietly awaken Jack Weaver. He was halfway there when the skitter of claws on wood alerted him a dog was coming down the hall. A bound brought him to a dresser, and he hunkered beside it a heartbeat before the animal filled the doorway.

The mongrel was the size of a calf, with a brindled, shaggy coat. It surveyed the bedroom and was starting to turn when there was a snort from the bed.

"What the hell? What is the window doing open?"

The voice wasn't that of Jack or Molly Weaver; it was the voice of Luther Carson! The cabin didn't belong to the Weavers! Nate was in the wrong one! He heard the bed creak, and around the end of it shuffled the burly blacksmith in a nightshirt that hung down around his stout knees. Scratching himself, Carson shambled to the window and slammed it shut.

"What's that, dear?" Agatha roused, thick with sleep. "What's going on?"

"We forgot to close the window. Now that I'm up, I think I'll have a glass of milk. Would you like one?"

"No, thank you. Don't stay up long, though. You know how irritable you get when you don't have enough rest."

"Nag, nag, nag," Carson said, going off down the hall. The dog went with him.

Nate listened for Agatha's rhythmic breathing to resume, and when it did, he crabbed to the window, raised it high enough to fork his leg over the sill, and eased back out. Lowering the window again, he darted to the fence and was soon at the road, disappointed at the outcome.

He couldn't very well go from cabin to cabin searching for the Weavers. The risk of discovery was too great. As much as he would like to take them along, it was now out of the question.

Nate bent his steps toward Huntington Manor. He was abreast of the last homestead on the right when an ominous growl from behind the picket fence took him to ground once again. Too late. A pair of glittering eyes were fixed on him.

Hoping the dog would lose interest if he simply lay there, Nate bided his time. Time he didn't have to spare.

When the animal's growls elicited no reaction, the dog paced back and forth, trying to catch his scent on the wind. When that failed, it moved toward the cabin and roosted on the porch beside a rocking chair.

Nate crawled northward until he was far enough off to rise without being seen. The manor, the mercantile, and the stable were as quiet as they had been when he left. After pausing long enough to insure that Private Bell and the bloodhound were nowhere in the vicinity, he sprinted to the entrance and was inside in the blink of an eye.

Through the parlor, down the hall. Nate slowed at Ezriah's

room, the walls still resounding to his snores. A little farther, and Nate gripped the latch to Evelyn's door. He glanced over his shoulder, then opened it and stepped inside, saying, "I have bad news, I'm afraid."

"So do I, Mr. King."

Nate stopped dead. Perched on the edge of the bed was William Harrison Proctor. Nearby stood Sergeant Braddock. Private Yates was by the window, a cocked pistol in his right hand. "Where are my wife and daughter?"

"Safe," Colonel Proctor said. "Just down the hall in another room, being guarded by Private Danvers."

"You had no right—" Nate began, but New Eden's future governor wouldn't let him finish.

"Please, sir, no feeble protests. No mock indignation. We both know what you've been up to, and frankly, I had hoped for better. To skulk about in the middle of the night like a common footpad is reprehensible."

Rankled by the man's gall, Nate responded, "We can leave any damn time we want, Proctor."

"Would that it were true. Unfortunately, I have need of your services. Yours, and your wife's. Until such time as I no longer require them, none of you are going anywhere." Colonel Proctor jerked a thumb at the noncom. "Sergeant Braddock, would you relieve our guest of his guns? And his knife and tomahawk, while you're at it."

"Sorry, Mr. King," Braddock apologized as he warily stepped to one side so as not to get between Nate and Private Yates. Reaching around, he helped himself to the four pistols and the other weapons.

Raw fury pumped through Nate's veins. "You shouldn't have done this," he said. Were it not for the pistol leveled at his chest, he would have lit into Proctor like a berserk wolverine.

"I beg to differ," the colonel said. "New Eden's welfare

comes before all else. I will do anything—*anything*—to realize our dream of a new state. If that necessitates detaining you and your wife against your will for a while, so be it."

"There will be a reckoning," Nate declared.

Proctor chuckled. "Oh, please. Juvenile posturing is unbecoming. You are in no position to threaten me, no position to do other than what I require of you. Accept the inevitable, Mr. King, and your stay here will be more bearable."

Nate would never accept being deprived of his freedom, of being held a virtual prisoner. Proctor had broken the bounds of all propriety. "For your own sake, let us go before it's too late."

"Or what? You'll rise up in righteous wrath and slay us? Instead of indulging in threats you can't possibly carry out, you should be inquiring about the services I referred to. Or aren't you the least bit curious?"

"You'll tell me anyway."

"That I will. But I would rather do so as your friend than your enemy. I would rather you helped me willingly than under duress."

"That will never happen," Nate said. The man was unbelievably arrogant to think he could force others to do his bidding and not have them resent it.

"Why not? You said, yourself, we must take steps to protect ourselves from the Blackfoot Confederacy. To that end, I intend to have you scout the country to the north. If you see any sign of hostiles, you're to ride like the wind and warn us. In the meantime, we will fortify our defenses in case of a mass attack."

"And where will my wife and daughter be while I'm off scouting?"

Colonel Proctor grinned. "Why, right here at Huntington Manor. Your wife, Mr. King, is even more essential to my plans than you are. As a linguist, she will act as my interpreter at the peace council. She speaks half a dozen tongues, correct?"

Nate didn't answer, which struck the officer as humorous.

"Be petty if you wish. It won't change the inevitable. You will leave at first light. Sergeant Braddock will provide you with enough food to last eight to ten days, but you will not be permitted to take weapons. A frontiersman of your caliber should have no difficulty surviving without them."

"Not even my knife?"

"And have you sneak back here in the dead of night and slit my throat?" Proctor rejoined. "Now that I think about it, as an added measure I'll have a couple of my men tag along for the first day or so."

Nate's rage was potent enough to choke on. Were it not for Yates's pistol, he would gladly have thrown himself at the colonel and beaten him within an inch of his overbearing life.

"Try to put yourself in my boots," Proctor said. "Think of all the people who depend on me, whose lives rely on my judgment. Can you blame me for doing whatever I must to safeguard them?"

"You could have asked us."

"To what end? Both you and your wife had made your intention to leave tomorrow abundantly clear. I was content to wait until morning to impose my will, but when you snuck off, you forced my hand."

"You saw me leave?"

"Not I. Rufus. I'd instructed him to spend the night in the stable's hay loft and keep an eye on the manor. He was to report to me if he saw anything out of the ordinary."

Nate recalled the loft door being open when he snuck off, but he hadn't thought much of it at the time. Why should he have? Loft doors were routinely left open to air a stable out.

"I must say," Proctor remarked, "that woman of yours is a firebrand. Had it not been for the risk to your daughter, she would have assaulted us when we burst in on her. I saw it in her eyes. A desire to kill me. Can you imagine?"

Yes, Nate thought, *very easily*. "What about Ezriah Hampton?"

"The simpleton? What about him? He can stay as long as you do so long as he doesn't make a nuisance of himself." Proctor cocked his head. "Listen to him. It sounds as if he is sawing petrified wood. He's out to the world, and has no idea Sergeant Braddock entered his room a short while ago and relieved him of all his weapons."

"Ezriah won't like that."

"Do you honestly think I care? The doddering old fool is of less consequence to me than a fly. He's lucky I don't send him packing on general principles." Rising, Colonel Proctor moved toward the door, his hands behind his back. "Any last questions or comments before I bid you good night? I have a busy day ahead of me tomorrow and need more sleep."

"One last time. Let us go."

"When I am damn good and ready." Proctor waited while Private Yates and Sergeant Braddock circled past Nate, careful to keep out of his reach. "Scowling like that is most unbecoming. Make the best of the situation, Mr. King." He started to leave.

"I'd like to speak to Winona and Evelyn before you turn in."

"Request denied. They've quieted down, and I see no need to stir them up again. You can talk to them in the morning before you ride out."

"Is a glass of whiskey too much to ask for?" Nate said with a taunting smirk, and the ruse worked.

"At this late hour? What are you, a lush?" Colonel Proctor shrugged. "Very well. I'll send Thomas around. But be advised. Private Yates will be right outside, so don't try anything."

The door closed behind them and Nate began to pace like

a caged grizzly. Proctor was too sure of himself, too confident, and that bred carelessness. The colonel had made a mistake that would prove costly before the night was done.

Impatient for the manservant to arrive, Nate stopped often to listen for footsteps. When at last he heard them, he scooted to the chair in the corner and sat.

The next second Private Yates poked his head in. "Remember what the colonel said, mister. Don't get any ideas or you'll regret them. All the darkie has to do is holler and I'll be on you like a gator on a suckling pig. Got me?"

Yates withdrew and Thomas came in, carrying a silver tray. "You requested a whiskey, sir?"

Nate indicated the chest of drawers near the chair and Thomas brought the tray over and set it down. The manservant held the glass out to him but Nate shook his head and whispered, "I don't really want a drink, Thomas. I wanted to talk to you. You strike me as a decent man."

"Sir?"

"Do you know what has happened?"

Thomas glanced at the partly open door, then bent down. "I was the one who admitted Rufus to Colonel Proctor's bedchamber. I heard everything, sir."

"Do you approve?"

"Whether I do or not is irrelevant, Mr. King. I'm in no position to help."

"That's where you're wrong. I'd like for you to get a message to my wife."

"Private Danvers would never let me go near her. He's lounging out in front of their room, picking his teeth with a knife."

"He will if you say Colonel Proctor told you to look in on them and see if they require anything." Nate gripped the other's wrist. "Will you help us, Thomas? My family is in danger and you're my only hope. I'm asking you man to man."

87

Thomas blinked a few times. "Man to man," he said softly. "Do you know, Mr. King, that in all the years I've been indentured to Colonel Proctor, never once has he shown me a smidgen of the respect you and your family have. He always refers to me as his slave. His servant. His colored help. His Negro. But never a man. Never a human being."

"I can count on your help?"

"Yes, sir, but not for the reason you think." Thomas lowered his voice until it was barely audible. "I like your wife. She doesn't look down her nose at me like some of the other women do. So it's only right I warn you. You've got to get her out of here before Proctor lays his hands on her."

A cold chill rippled down Nate's spine and into the depths of his soul. "Before he does *what?*"

Thomas spoke rapidly. "Colonel Proctor isn't the paragon of virtue his men believe him to be. He has a weakness. A powerful weakness. He's fond of the ladies, Mr. King. Can't keep his hands off them. You've seen Harriet, his personal maid, how he has her dress, how she dotes on him? He took her for the first time when she was only fourteen and she's been his bedmate ever since."

"She doesn't mind?"

"No, she likes being a kept woman. But even if she did, what could she do? She's a slave. She has no rights. Even her own body isn't hers to do with as she sees fit. Colonel Proctor owns her lock, stock, and barrel."

A slight noise in the hall caused both of them to glance sharply around. When nothing came of it, Thomas went on just as swiftly.

"Harriet isn't the only woman the colonel diddles. Several of the wives come visit him from time to time when their husbands are off on patrol. It's been going on for years but none of them suspect." Thomas radiated disgust. "He also lusted after Mrs. Weaver but she refused to give in. That's why she and her husband were running away."

"And now you think Proctor has designs on Winona?"

"I don't think he does," Thomas said. "I know he does. I saw him looking at Mrs. King with that peculiar sort of look he gets when he wants a woman real bad. If you go riding off into the mountains tomorrow, she'll be at his mercy. He'll concoct an excuse to get her alone and force himself on her."

"Over my dead body," Nate growled, and it was all he could do to keep from charging out into the hall to hunt Proctor down. Placing his hand on Thomas's shoulder, he said, "Listen. Here is what you need to do. . . ."

Chapter Seven

Winona King prided herself on her self-control. From an early age Shoshone girls were taught they must always keep a tight rein on their emotions. That in addition to mastering the many skills involved in maintaining a lodge and rearing a family, they must master themselves and be a credit to their husbands and their tribe. They were expected to bear pain and discomfort stoically, as the men did. They were expected to show the courage of a warrior, and lay down their lives in defense of their village and their families, if need be.

Winona's mother had also impressed on her that a woman must never give in to her baser impulses. A woman should not be petty, must avoid being shrewish, and must not bicker with her husband over trifles. Above all, a woman must control her innermost feelings and never, ever give in to anger. Anger was a bitter venom, eating at the spirit. It destroyed peace of mind and the harmony of a lodge.

By and large, Winona had lived up to her mother's expectations. Her husband, her children, and everyone who knew her continually complimented her on her poise, on her calm self-assurance. They rarely saw her upset, seldom saw her mad.

But Winona was mad now. So mad she could not collect her thoughts. So mad her body was hot with rage. Mad enough to kill with her bare hands.

The object of her wrath was William Harrison Proctor. Along with Braddock, Yates, and Danvers, he had barged into Evelyn's room while the two of them were seated on the bed talking, catching her unawares. She had lunged for her rifle but Yates had snatched it. When she tried to draw a pistol, Braddock had pinned her arms while Danvers had confiscated her weapons.

William Harrison Proctor had done nothing except stand there and smirk. After she was unarmed and Braddock released her, Proctor had taken a seat and prattled on about his glorious plans for New Eden and the crucial part she was to play as his interpreter.

Winona flatly refused to help him.

Proctor's moon face had rotated toward Evelyn and his flat eyes had lit with menace. "Are you sure I can't convince you to change your mind, my dear?"

At that moment Winona decided she was going to kill him.

Proctor had talked some of his military career, and from time to time Winona caught his eyes devouring her. But he always stifled his lust when she looked at him, as devious as he was degenerate.

Then, at gunpoint, Winona and Evelyn had been marched to another room so Proctor could arrange a suitable reception for Nate. She had balked until Proctor threatened to have her hog-tied if she didn't comply.

So now here Winona was, seething in rare rage and pacing the floor while her daughter lay curled on the double bed. The murmur of brief conversation outside the door preceded a light knock and a kindly voice saying, "Mrs. King? It's Thomas. May I come in?"

"By all means," Winona said. The manservant had impressed her as being considerate and decent. He might be willing to help.

"Who's that, Ma?" Evelyn said, sitting up and rubbing her eyes. "Is it Pa? Is he back yet?"

"It is not your father, little one. Go back to sleep."

Thomas entered bearing a silver tray with nothing on it. Behind him stood Private Danvers, a stocky militiaman who wore a perpetual frown. "No shenanigans, lady. The colonel sent him to see if you want anything."

Winona looked at Thomas, who wore the strangest expression. "No, thank you," she said. "We are fine."

"Are you sure, madam?" Thomas said, and then silently mouthed several words.

Winona was at a loss. He was trying to tell her something but she had no notion of what it was. "Well, I suppose we could do with a glass of—" She was about to say "water" but they had a water pitcher in the room, so instead she said, "Juice, if you have any. Or milk if you do not."

Thomas grinned. "Juice it is. I'll be back in five minutes." He winked at her, then departed as if his britches were on fire.

Private Danvers closed the door after him.

"Thomas didn't say what kind of juice," Evelyn said, sinking back down and closing her eyes. "I hope it's grape. I've only had it on that trip we took to Kansas City, but I love grape juice."

Winona didn't care what it was. She just wanted to get Thomas alone for a minute so she could ask him to relay a message to Nate. Continuing to pace, she eagerly awaited his return and nearly jumped when the latch rasped without warning.

"Here you go, Mrs. King. Apple cider." Thomas had brought

two tall glasses. He set the tray on the small mahogany table by the bed. "Help yourselves."

Private Danvers was in the doorway. "Leave it and go," he said.

"Sorry, sir, but Colonel Proctor was quite specific. I'm to wait for them to finish and take the empty glasses back with me. Something about not letting them have sharp objects."

"What? The colonel is afraid the squaw will bust one and try to cut me?" Danvers snorted. "I'd like to see her try." He backed out into the hall, saying testily, "I'll be right outside. Holler if she so much as looks at you crosswise."

Thomas held out a glass. "It's part of a batch we brought from North Carolina. I think you'll find it quite delicious."

"Thank you." As Winona reached for it, the manservant bent toward her and whispered urgently.

"Your husband sent me with a message. They are holding him in your daughter's room. He says the three of you must escape as soon as possible."

"I could not agree more," Winona whispered, watching the doorway in case Danvers popped back in.

"He told me to ask you a question. The question makes no sense to me but he said you would understand." Thomas paused. "Are your possibles intact?"

The cryptic question was an allusion to Winona's possibles bag, the leather pouch in which frontiersmen traditionally kept their fire steel and flint, their sewing kit, their whetstone, and other personal effects. She knew why he had asked, and she answered, "Yes, it is."

"Good. Then I'm to tell you to wait a bit after I've gone and pound on the west wall as hard as you can. That will be his signal."

"I understand."

"I'm glad you do," Thomas said. "I asked him what it was all about but he told me it's best if I don't know."

David Thompson

A shadow moved across the doorway. Winona tipped the glass to her lips, and over its brim she saw Danvers peering in at them. He grunted, then stepped back into the hall. "This is delicious," she said for his benefit.

Evelyn sidled across the bed on her knees. "How about me, Ma?" she said, so tired she could hardly keep her eyes open. "I'd like some, too."

"Here you go, little miss." Thomas gave her the other glass, and leaned toward Winona again. "Your weapons have been taken to the drawing room in the east wing. It's the second door on the left past the parlor."

"I am grateful for your help," Winona said, touching his hand. "Sincerely grateful."

"I feel good about it my own self," Thomas whispered. "This is the first time in my life I've ever stood up to the colonel, the first time I've ever stood up for what I believe is right." He looked down at himself in reproach. "I should have done it decades ago. I guess when a body is trod on long enough, it gets used to being a rug."

"Will this cause you any trouble?" Winona thought to ask.

"No, ma'am. Your husband says they'll never suspect I had a hand in it." Thomas shrugged. "Frankly, I don't much care if they do. I'm tired of having to lick the colonel's boots, tired of being bossed and prodded, tired of being less than a man."

"Come with us, then."

Thomas's eyes lit like candles, and just as quickly the light faded. "Would that I could, Mrs. King. I've thought about running, about taking the underground railway to the North and freedom. But as much as I long to, I can't bring myself to do it."

"We would help you go wherever you wanted," Winona offered.

"Why, that's about the sweetest thing anyone ever said to me," Thomas said huskily. "But I can't. I just can't." He paused. "My daughter would never go with me, and I could never abandon her."

"Aletha is your daughter?"

"No, ma'am. Harriet is."

"Oh."

A wan smile curled Thomas's thick lips. "Her mother died when she was little. A runaway wagon hit her and broke her neck. I had to do the best I could raising Harriet on my own. I tried to instill values in the girl, tried to teach her to live a life that would make her mother proud. But Harriet was always headstrong. Always had to do things her way. Always knew better than I did what was best for her."

"I'm sorry, Thomas."

"Not nearly as sorry as I am. She grew into a pretty thing, and Colonel Proctor was quick to take notice. He had her brought to his bedroom one night when she wasn't but a few years older than your girl, and she's been his private tramp ever since."

"She must have her reasons," Winona said.

"Such as they are. Harriet likes to be treated as if she's an important lady. She likes nice clothes and good food and a warm bed at night. And the colonel gives her just enough to keep her under his thumb. She thinks he's going to make a free woman of her one day, and take her as his wife. But she's living in a fool's paradise. He'll string her along until he loses interest, until her looks start to fade and he moves on to someone younger and prettier. That's how these things work, only she's too blinded by her own pride to see it."

"I can not begin to imagine how you must feel," Winona sympathized. To be owned by another person, to have every facet of his life dictated by another, to see his own child molested and manipulated by a lecherous monster—her heart went out to him and she fervently wished there was some way she could help him. Then it hit her. There was. She could go through with the decision she had made.

"I almost joined Turner's revolt a few years back," Thomas remarked, and when he saw she did not understand, he said, "Nat Turner. Back in thirty-one he led a revolt against slavery up in Virginia. He and about thirty slaves killed some fifty whites. It took three thousand men to track him down. They hung him, of course, but it got a lot of black people to thinking how things could be if slavery was abolished, like some folks in the North want."

"Maybe it will be abolished one day."

Thomas grew wistful. "If so, I hope to God I live long enough to see that day come. My father was a slave, and his father before him. I would be the first to taste freedom, the first to live as I want to live rather than as others demand I do." He chuckled. "I would think I had died and gone to heaven."

Private Danvers stepped into the bedroom. "How long does it take to drink a glass of juice?"

Winona downed the rest of hers in several gulps. "We're about done," she said, handing the glass to Thomas. "Thank you. For everything."

Evelyn dawdled over hers, sipping slowly and smacking her lips.

"Hurry it up, girl," Private Danvers griped.

Scrunching her face at him, Evelyn upended the last of the juice. "You're not very nice," she said as she gave the glass up. "I don't think I like you very much."

"I'll try not to lose any sleep over it," Danvers countered, and stepped aside so Thomas could depart. In his annoyed state, he slammed the door after them.

Winona promptly sat on the bed and opened her possibles bag. Slipping her hand inside, she found the objects she was after.

"What are you doing, Ma?"

"Our captors made a mistake they will regret," Winona said. "They took my rifle and pistols and knife, but they did not think to look in here." Not that there was any reason they should. Full-sized pistols and knives were so big and bulky that carrying them in a possibles bag wasn't practical. But a possibles bag was large enough to contain, say, a derringer. Winona pulled hers out and set about loading it.

Evelyn tittered, then covered her mouth and glanced at the door. "I plumb forgot. Pa and you each took one from the *Sagah-lee.*"

Winona extracted the small ramrod from its housing under the short barrel. The derringer was a Henry Derringer single-shot .41 caliber with walnut stock. Almost small enough to fit into the palm of her hand, it was only effective at extremely close range. She loaded it swiftly, replaced the ramrod, and rose. "You must listen to me, little one, and you must listen closely."

"I always do, Ma."

"We are about to try to escape. You must do exactly as I say. If the guard tries to shoot me, you must drop to the floor so you are not hit."

"If he tries to shoot you, I'll kick him in the shins."

"No, you will do as I have told you."

Winona stepped to the west wall. Bracing herself, she hauled off and pounded it as hard as she could, then lowered her hands at her sides, the derringer concealed by her leg.

Not a second later the door swung inward and Private Danvers snapped, "What the hell was that noise?"

"I hit the wall," Winona admitted.

"What for?"

"I am mad," Winona said, hoping to lure him farther in. "Mad at Colonel Proctor, mad at all of you."

"Should I shed a tear now or later?" Danvers taunted. He

took another step and gestured. "Get away from there, and stay away. No more pounding or you won't like what I do."

"That works both ways, Private."

"How so, squaw?"

Winona pointed the derringer at his face. "Raise your arms over your head."

Private Danvers did no such thing. His right hand was inches from the holster on his hip, and he flexed his fingers, declaring, "The colonel will have me whipped if I let you get away. So I'm not about to. Make this easy on both of us and drop your gun."

"If you think I will not shoot you, you are mistaken," Winona affirmed.

"You'll try," Danvers said. "But if I move fast enough, even at this range you might miss. I'd rather take my chances with you than with the colonel."

Winona did not want to shoot if she could help it. The shot was bound to be heard and bring others on the run. "You are willing to die to avoid a whipping?"

"Sounds crazy, doesn't it? But that's the way it is." And with that, Private Danvers stabbed a hand at the flap.

Thirty seconds earlier, in the room at the west end of the hallway, Nate heard the thump he had been waiting for. Thomas had gotten word to Winona. His hand was already on the latch, and he quietly opened the door and peeked out.

Private Yates had heard the thump, too, and had taken a couple of paces along the corridor. Beyond him, Private Danvers opened a door to another bedroom and disappeared within.

A quick step brought Nate to Yates. Jamming the muzzle of the derringer against the back of the militiaman's neck, he said, "If you so much as twitch, you're dead."

Yates imitated a sapling. "Son of a bitch! Where did you get a gun?"

"Had it in my possibles bag," Nate answered while reaching down to snag the North Carolinian's flintlock. Smoothly jerking it out, he reversed his grip and brought the hardwood stock crashing down on top of the private's skull. Yates folded like an accordion, uttering a low groan, and Nate was past him before he hit the floor, racing to the open doorway and reaching it in time to hear his wife say, "You are willing to die to avoid a whipping?"

"Sounds crazy, doesn't it? But that's the way it is."

Nate saw Private Danvers make a stab for his holster. A long bound brought Nate near enough, and he whipped the flintlock up and around, crashing it onto Danvers's head with the force of a toppling tree. Danvers fell in a disjointed pile, his limbs askew, his body briefly quaking as if he were having a fit.

"Pa!" Evelyn squealed, and was off the bed in a flash. She hurled herself against him, wrapping her slender arms around his legs. "They didn't hurt you!"

"We must hurry," Nate said. "Help your mother tie this man up while I take care of the other one." Smiling at Winona, he ran back out—and nearly collided with a grizzled bundle of bone and sinew who was yawning wide enough to swallow Long's Peak while scratching his head in befuddlement.

"What's all the ruckus out here? Can't a fella get a wink of sleep without everyone carrying on?" Ezriah Hampton lowered his hand to the empty scabbard at his waist, and recoiled as if he had been slapped. "What the blazes? Where's my fancy sword? And my pistols? I still had them on me when I fell asleep."

"Proctor and his men took them," Nate said, and launched into a brief explanation of all that had transpired since the gathering broke up.

"The scoundrels stole into my room while I slept?" Ezriah said, bristling like a porcupine. "Holding you and your wife against your will is one thing, but when they steal a person's weapons, they've gone too far!"

"Not so loud!" Nate scolded. "Do you want to bring the whole bunch down on our heads when all we have are a couple of pistols and derringers?"

"Bring the vermin on!" Ezriah said, sweeping the cloak back over his shoulder. Suddenly stiffening, he grabbed his leather bag and shoved a hand inside. "Thank God! My gold coins are still here! What kind of idiots steal a few weapons but overlook a small fortune?"

"Watch the hallway while I take care of something." Nate dashed to Yates and dragged the soldier into Evelyn's former bedroom. A hunting knife on the man's belt gave him the means to cut strips from the quilt and use them to securely bind both wrists and ankles. He also stuffed a strip into the private's mouth.

Winona and Evelyn were waiting with Ezriah when Nate emerged. The old trapper was fully awake now, and fit to chew nails.

"Damn Proctor, anyhow! And here I was beginning to admire the man! I say we find him and gut him like a fish!"

"First we find our weapons," Winona said. Once that was done, she would attend to William Harrison Proctor personally.

Nate shoved his derringer into Ezriah's hand. "Take this. Stay close behind us and give a holler if anyone spots us."

"This puny little gun?" Hampton said. "I can sneeze harder than this thing can shoot."

"Hold on to it anyway until we reclaim our own." Nate moved toward the parlor. In the dark it had an empty, ominous air, which he chalked up to nerves. He was worried sick one of the staff or a militiaman would blunder onto them.

The foreboding portrait of Colonel Proctor gazed down at them with paint-glazed eyes as they crossed to the hallway opposite. The only sound was the *tick-tick-tick* of the ornate grandfather clock.

Winona remembered Thomas's instruction. "The second room on the left, husband," she whispered.

Nate nodded. He eased into the corridor, only to freeze at the sound of a door opening farther down. "Back!" he whispered, and flung himself to the rear, pushing his wife and daughter and the trapper ahead of him. No sooner were they around the corner than the pad of feet forewarned him someone was approaching.

"Hide!" Nate hissed. He pointed at the sofa, and the others dashed toward it. As they ducked from view, he sprang to the side of the grandfather clock and pressed his back to the wall.

None too soon. Into the parlor sashayed Harriet, her maid's uniform in disarray. Giggling, she made a beeline for the liquor cabinet, opened it, and after studying the labels, selected a bottle.

Harriet started toward the east hall but stopped after a few steps, giggled again, and opened it. "What's a few sips on the side?" she said aloud. Gluing her full lips to the mouth, she swigged like a sailor, her throat bobbing as she chugged an eighth of the contents in half as many seconds.

"Nice and smooth," Harriet said. She capped the bottle, tucked it under her left arm, and ambled into the hall, her bottom jiggling like a puppet with a broken string.

Nate realized that if she was awake, so was Proctor. Side-stepping to the corner, he aligned his right eye with the edge and saw Harriet prance to a door across from the dining room and enter without bothering to knock or announce herself. From its confines wafted gruff male laughter, laughter muffled when the door swung shut.

Winona had brought Evelyn over. "We must get out of

101

here," she stressed. As much to thwart Proctor as to spare her daughter any more unseemly displays. Women who pandered their bodies had always perplexed her. She held herself in too high esteem to ever stoop to indulging in carnal passion for the sheer sake of fleeting pleasure, and she could never understand females who did.

"Where's Ezriah?" Nate asked, then spied the trapper over by the liquor cabinet, helping himself. "What are you doing?" he whispered.

"What does it look like, hoss?" Hampton responded. "Helping myself."

"Not now! Get over here!"

Ezriah took a silver flask from a shelf, uncorked it, and sniffed. Pleased, he indulged in several hearty swallows, sighed with contentment, and slid the flask under his coat. "Got what I needed. Lead on, big man."

The second door on the left was closed. Nate gripped the latch, then paused, wondering if there were militiamen in the room. There was only one way to find out. Squaring his shoulders, he barreled on in.

Furniture and drapes, and that was it. On a settee were the weapons, exactly as Thomas had said.

Nate checked each of the four pistols before sliding them under his belt. He shoved the ivory-handled knife into its sheath on his right hip, placed the tomahawk on his left, and picked up the Hawken. "We'll go out through the front so the bloodhounds won't catch wind of us—"

"No," Winona said. She was armed again. Now no one, not even her beloved husband, would stay her hand.

"No?"

"We are not leaving until I have killed William Proctor."

Nate was too dumbfounded to stop her when she moved toward the door. His wife had never been bloodthirsty by nature. For her to imperil their lives to get revenge was so uncharacteristic of her, he didn't find his voice until she was out of reach. "Wait! Let's talk this over."

Winona wasn't inclined to do any such thing. The time for talk was past. She boldly stepped into the hall, and immediately regretted being so rash when she beheld Harriet a dozen feet away.

Huntington Manor pealed to a shriek of alarm.

Chapter Eight

"The Kings! The Kings are loose!" Harriet shrieked at the top of her lungs. An empty glass was in her left hand, and she flung it at them as she whirled toward the room she had disappeared into earlier.

Winona was fleeter of foot. Whipping her rifle in an arc, she slammed the stock into the side of Harriet's head, felling her like a poled mule. A spurt of speed brought her to the room William Harrison Proctor was in just as the door slammed in her face. She gripped the latch and heard a bolt being thrown. In exasperation, Winona threw her shoulder against the door but it was solid oak and withstood her attempt to smash through. Guttural laughter on the other side incensed her into hurling herself at the door again. Then a strong hand fell on her shoulder and she was pulled back.

"What are you doing?" Nate had never seen his wife so enraged. "That scream will bring others! Soon we'll have the whole settlement down on our head. We have to get out of here!"

104

"Proctor must die!" Winona said, tearing free. She threw her shoulder against the panel once more, with the same result. "Help me, husband! Please!"

Nate thought they were making a terrible mistake. But he had never been one to refuse his wife anything. Lowering his shoulder, he drove against the door like a human battering ram. There was a resounding crash but the door stood firm. He drew back to try again. Suddenly the manor rocked to the boom of a shot, and wood slivers flew every which way. A slug had ripped through the center of the door, narrowly missing them. Nate jumped back, hauling her with him.

"No! We must kill Proctor!" Winona did not want to leave the lecher alive to prey on other girls as he had done to Harriet.

"Another time, maybe, beloved," Nate said. Elsewhere in the manor feet were pounding, and outside someone was bellowing. He started toward the dining room, pulling her along. Since there was no longer any need for stealth, it didn't matter whether they went out the front or the back.

Winona resisted a few moments longer, until the crack of a pistol outdoors brought her to her senses. It was a signal. The militiamen would rouse out of bed and converge on the manor in force. Her husband was right.

"Are you okay, Ma?"

Winona looked down into her daughter's upturned face, lined with fear for her welfare. "Do not fret, little one," she said, taking Evelyn's hand. "I lost my head for a bit but I am fine now."

Ezriah brought up the rear, muttering to himself as usual. "Consarndest family I ever did see! A woman who thinks she's a warrior, and a man who goes around being more mushy than one of them playactors."

The dining room was dark and deserted. Nate flew across to the door at the rear and down a narrow hall into the kitchen. Two large stoves took up most of the room. They passed a hardwood counter, a washbasin, scores of cooking utensils, and a storage closet.

The door to the outside was barred.

"Watch our backs, Ezriah," Nate said. Removing the bar, he cracked the door wide enough to scan the yard. The bloodhounds were in an uproar. Agitated by all the commotion, they brayed and threw themselves against the fence.

Nate didn't see Private Bell anywhere. Motioning, he jogged to the right along the wall. They needed horses, and the nearest place to acquire some was the stable. In the manor men were yelling. One voice was Colonel Proctor's, roaring orders from the sound of it. Nate ducked under a lit window.

"Halt! Halt or I'll fire!"

Nate glanced back. Private Bell was at the far end of Huntington Manor, a rifle tucked to his shoulder, the bloodhound at his side.

"Go to hell!" Ezriah hollered. Snapping up his Kentucky, he fired first. In his haste he missed, but it had the effect of compelling Bell to seek cover around the corner. Cackling, Ezriah said, "That'll teach the buzzard!"

Nate saw a blur of movement close to the ground. Private Bell had sicced the bloodhound on them, and the dog was a molten streak, loping in long, fluid bounds. Even as he spotted it, the animal vented a ferocious growl. He brought up his Hawken but Ezriah blundered into his line of fire.

"Ma!" Evelyn yelled.

Winona had seen it, too. Extending her rifle, she fixed a bead on the creature's chest, curled back the hammer, and fired. The ball sped true. The dog tumbled head over tail for eight to ten feet and came to rest on its side, as limp as a wet rag.

Nate pushed on. Now two of their rifles were empty and they couldn't afford the time to reload. Reaching the corner, he checked before he strode into the open, and it was well he did.

Rushing toward the manor from the stable was big, brawny Rufus, holding a pitchfork. He had on overalls and boots but no shirt, and his huge chest bulged with muscles. Throwing a side door wide, he plunged inside, shouting, "Colonel Proctor! Colonel Proctor! Where are you at?"

"Now!" Nate said, and broke for the stable. He matched his pace to that of Winona, who, in turn, went no faster than Evelyn was able to run. Ezriah trailed them, mumbling something about "turtles and snails."

The corral attached to the stable was empty. Nate assumed the animals had been taken inside for the night. When he came to the double doors, he flung the left one open. Sure enough, the stalls were filled. Some of the horses nickered nervously at the intrusion. "Pick one and climb on," he said.

"What about saddles and saddle blankets?" Ezriah asked.

"It would take too long." Nate moved down the center aisle. "We'll ride bareback."

"I hate doing that," Ezriah complained. "I get so sore I can't sit for a week."

"Would you rather be so dead you can't sit at all?" Nate countered.

"Good point, sonny."

"We do need bridles, though," Nate said. There had to be a tack room, but in the gloom he couldn't locate it. Toward the back, he figured.

"Listen, Pa!" Evelyn abruptly cried. "Do you hear what I hear?"

Nate paused. To the west hooves drummed. Militiamen were galloping toward Huntington Manor. "Damn!" He hadn't expected them to show up so soon. But then, they *were* soldiers, men trained to respond swiftly in a crisis. Before long the area would be swarming with them.

Winona was seeking a suitable mount for Evelyn. The first stall contained a skittish stallion, the next a large bay. The third held a mare, and Winona was about to open the door when she realized the mare was swollen like a pumpkin. Any day now the foal was due.

Nate thought he espied an opening that might be the tack room but as he started toward it a rumbling challenge filled the stable.

"What do you folks think you're doin?"

Rufus was at the double doors, pitchfork in hand. In the dark he loomed like an ebony carven statue.

Ezriah was closest. Facing around, he said, "What does it look like we're doing, genius? We're getting set to light a shuck. Do yourself a favor and put down that fork before you get hurt."

"I can't let you steal the colonel's animals," Rufus said. "Give up while you can or you're the ones who will be hurt."

From under Ezriah's cloak a pistol materialized. "You've got more muscles than most ten men, but muscles don't make you bulletproof. So why don't you toddle along back to your lord and master and tell him we'll do this again sometime when we're all out of our minds?"

"Huh?" Rufus said.

"Scoot. Skedaddle. Get lost." Ezriah waved the pistol. "Go play in the kennel with the bloodhounds."

"You're pokin' fun at me," Rufus grated. "And I don't like it much when folks poke fun at me."

"And I don't like being poked, period." Ezriah steadied the flintlock. "Drop it, or so help me God, I'll drop you."

Nate rushed back down the aisle and stepped in front of the trapper. "No. He's only doing what he thinks is right. Don't kill him."

"Are you addlepated?" Ezriah responded. "Look at him! He'll stick us if we don't put a window in his skull."

Rufus was gliding toward them with the pitchfork ready to thrust. "Drop your guns! I'm takin' you to the colonel."

Nate had to marvel at the man's devotion to someone who owned him. "Don't make us shoot. Our quarrel isn't with you."

"And I ain't got no quarrel with you, white man," Rufus said, planting himself a few yards off. "But I can't let you escape. The colonel wouldn't like that."

"Is he worth dying for, boy?" Ezriah said.

"I ain't your boy, mister," Rufus declared. "And it ain't him I'm doing it for. It's so I can have a night with Harriet."

"Harriet?" Winona had been content to stay out of it until that moment. Her husband and the trapper were between her and the black, so she sidled to the left to where she could see him clearly. "What does she have to do with it?"

"I'm powerful fond of her, lady. The colonel, he promised I could have her one day if'n I'm real good and don't get him mad at me. Maybe this will be the day."

Winona remembered Thomas telling her how Proctor would cast Harriet aside when he tired of her. She remembered the tears in Thomas's eyes, the sorrow in his voice, and she drew a pistol and put a bullet into Rufus's left thigh.

The stableman collapsed with a howl, his big hands pressed over the spurting hole, the pitchfork forgotten beside him. "You shot me! You done shot me!"

Nate was just as astounded. He didn't know what to make of Winona's behavior. She had never been so coldhearted, so merciless. It was as if he were married to a whole new person. "Why?" he asked.

Ezriah laughed. "Hell, I can answer that one. Your missus has bigger oysters than you do, hoss."

Clenching a fist, Nate shook it in the oldster's nose. "Remember Latham? One of these days that mouth of yours will earn you a fat lip."

"The truth hurts, doesn't it?" Ezriah said, and guffawed.

Out in the night hooves hammered, approaching at a rapid clip, four or five horses from the sound of things. Nate spun toward the rear. "Out the rear!" he cried. Rufus had delayed them just long enough to prevent them from helping themselves to mounts. Their only recourse now was to flee on foot.

Rufus twisted toward the double doors and cupped a bloody hand to his mouth. "In here! They're in here!"

Nate's temper was at the boiling point. Taking two swift steps, he kicked the stableman flush on the jaw and Rufus sprawled onto his stomach, dazed but not quite unconscious.

"I see your wife is rubbing off on you," Ezriah said.

Grabbing him, Nate shoved the trapper down the aisle. "Run or they'll catch us!"

He kept one eye on the double doors but no one appeared and within moments they were at the back. Most stables had a rear entrance and this one was no exception. Spread before them were acres of high grass sprinkled by stands of trees. A mile and a half off were the mountains. "Go!" he urged. "I'll cover you!"

A horse whinnied out in front as they sprinted into the grass. Nate heard hard voices, heard someone say, "Rufus! Rufus! Snap out of it! Where the hell did they go?"

Nate guessed they had maybe sixty seconds, if that. He overtook the others, Ezriah huffing and puffing like a broken steam engine, Evelyn striving her utmost not to slow them down.

A stone's throw to the northeast were some cottonwoods. "There!" Nate said, veering toward them. He covered another ten yards, glancing repeatedly over his shoulder. Motion at the front of the stable was his cue to wrap his arms around Winona and Evelyn and pull them down beside him, saying, "They're coming!"

Ezriah sagged onto his knees, gasping for breath. "It's all that food I ate," he husked. "I feel heavy as a whale."

Nate was only interested in their pursuers. Four riders swept around the stable and drew rein. Sergeant Braddock was in the lead, with Privates Stuart, Mitchell, and Timmons. "Spread out!" the noncom commanded. "They can't have gotten far! Don't forget, the colonel wants them alive if possible!"

Ezriah reached for a pistol, saying, "I'd like to see them try!"

"No!" Nate whispered, jerking the old trapper to the ground. He had no guarantee the militiamen wouldn't shoot back, and in the dark Winona or Evelyn might take a bullet. "We don't fire unless they do."

"You're downright pitiful, you know that?" Ezriah grumped. "If you'd been George Washington, the British would still run this country."

"Quiet!"

The quartet were fanning out at a brisk walk, Stuart to the south, Braddock and Mitchell bearing east, Timmons riding almost straight toward them.

"I can drop him easy," Ezriah whispered.

"Not unless I say so."

Winona had an arm around Evelyn, shielding her daughter with her own body. She regretted not being able to confront Proctor, and promised herself that if they survived, she would return one day soon to either slay him or convince him to part with Thomas and Harriet. She would bring along her cousin Touch The Clouds and a couple of dozen Shoshone warriors to help persuade him.

Private Timmons was forty feet out, looking right and left, a rifle slanted across his thighs. "Did you hear they shot Old Blue?" he hollered.

"No, it was Young Blue," Private Mitchell responded. "Yates told me the squaw did it. Shot him plumb in the brisket."

Sergeant Braddock twisted in the saddle. "Not another word, you jackasses! We can't hear anything with the two of you jawing."

"Sorry, Sarge," Timmons said.

Nate sighted down his Hawken. Another ten feet or so and the militiaman was bound to spot them. But just at that juncture, to the south, Private Stuart yipped.

"Over here! I see something moving! I think it's them! It's them!"

Braddock, Mitchell, and Timmons reined their animals around and applied their spurs, and in no time the night had swallowed them.

"To the trees," Nate said, rising. Capricious fate had granted a temporary reprieve and they had to make the most of it.

"Who did that man see, Pa?" Evelyn asked. "It sure wasn't us."

Nate recalled the deer in the road. "It could be anything. Run, run as hard as you can, and don't look back."

A great hubbub arose at the manor. Torches had been brought, and in their flickering glow over a dozen figures milled, some in dresses.

As soon as the cottonwoods closed around them, Nate turned and scoured the valley. Dawn was five or six hours off yet. By then they should be well up in the mountains. The New Edenites would expect them to try to break out through the pass to the east or the notch to the west, and would post militiamen to stop them. But it had been his experience that there were many routes over any given range; all he had to do was find another.

"We shouldn't stay here long," Winona mentioned. Another island of trees to the north was larger and offered thicker cover.

"Give me a bit," Ezriah said, a hand to his side. "I've got a godawful pain. It's like someone is gouging me with a spike."

"I can carry you," Nate suggested.

"You do and I'll bite your damn nose off. I'm not no kid. I

Join the Western Book Club
and GET 4 FREE* BOOKS NOW!
A $19.96 VALUE!

Yes! I want to subscribe
to the Western Book Club.

Please send me my **4 FREE* BOOKS**. I have enclosed $2.00 for shipping/handling. Each month I'll receive the four newest Leisure Western selections to preview for 10 days. If I decide to keep them, I will pay the Special Members Only discounted price of just $3.36 each, a total of $13.44, plus $2.00 shipping/handling ($22.30 US in Canada). This is a **SAVINGS OF AT LEAST $6.00** off the bookstore price. There is no minimum number of books I must buy, and I may cancel the program at any time. In any case, the **4 FREE* BOOKS** are mine to keep.

*In Canada, add $5.00 shipping/handling per order for the first shipment. For all future shipments to Canada, the cost of membership is $22.30 US, which includes shipping and handling. (All payments must be made in US dollars.)

NAME: _____

ADDRESS: _____

CITY: _____ **STATE:** _____

COUNTRY: _____ **ZIP:** _____

TELEPHONE: _____

E-MAIL: _____

SIGNATURE: _____

If under 18, Parent or Guardian must sign. Terms, prices, and conditions subject to change. Subscription subject to acceptance. Dorchester Publishing reserves the right to reject any order or cancel any subscription.

can manage on my own perfectly fine if you'll give me a minute to catch my breath."

Evelyn wagged a finger. "You sure do use a lot of cuss words, Mr. Hampton."

"When you get as old and cranky as me, you'll use a lot of cuss words, too, missy," Ezriah said. "Everyone my age does."

"Not everyone," Evelyn said. "We have a friend called Shakespeare McNair, and he hardly ever cusses."

"McNair?" Ezriah said. "That old coon is still around? Hell, he must be pushing a hundred."

"He has hair as white as snow," Evelyn mentioned. "Just like you."

"We're the last of our kind, sprout. He and I were two of the first white men to set foot in the Rockies. Me, I went and got myself taken prisoner by the *Sa-gah-lee* and spent a good chunk of my life as their captive. What's McNair been up to?"

"He lives in a nice cabin and has a pretty Flathead, Blue Water Woman, as his wife. We go to visit them now and then. He doesn't get around as much as he used to."

"At our age we're lucky if we have the energy to pick our nose," Ezriah said. "Growing old is a curse, girl. It's God's way of punishing us for what Adam did in the Garden. Our bodies wither and weaken until we can't hardly get about, yet deep inside we still feel as young as we were when we were your age. It's cruel, is what it is. And puts the lie to those Bible-thumpers who claim the Almighty is all sweetness and light."

"Pa says God is never cruel to folks. He says we bring a lot of bad things down on our own heads."

Ezriah chortled. "No offense, dearie, but your pa ain't exactly brimming with brains. He got himself caught by the *Sa-gah-lee*, too didn't he? And then he went and got all of us into this mess."

Evelyn's jaw jutted out. "Don't talk about my pa like that, Mr. Hampton. He's the smartest and best man there is."

"Sure, girl. Sure."

Nate had been listening for hoofbeats or any other sign that Braddock and the others were returning. The clamor at the manor had grown louder, with considerable activity over by the mercantile, too. What that was all about he couldn't say. "Enough rest," he told the trapper. "Let's keep going."

Staying low, the four of them dog-trotted to the next cluster of vegetation. Heavy thickets had to be negotiated, a tricky proposition in the shadowy murk. Nate's face and hands bore half a dozen scratches and nicks when he stopped at the far edge of the stand and hunkered. His confidence they could elude the militiamen was mounting.

Another open tract of grass separated them from broad woodland. The moon, Nate observed, would soon disappear behind some clouds, providing them with a welcome mantle of darkness. He mentioned it to the others. "We'll wait. It shouldn't be more than a minute or two."

Ezriah was holding his side again. "Too bad it's not ten," he said. "You might have to go on without me."

Winona placed her hand on his shoulder. "Are you that bad off?"

"It feels as if I was gored by a buffalo." Ezriah took a few deep breaths, and groaned. "Life. Got to love it."

"What do you mean, Mr. Hampton?" Evelyn whispered.

"Every time things are going our way, life ups and kicks us in the teeth. I used to think real happiness was a sham, that the only reason we were put on this earth was to suffer, grow old, and die."

Winona gave him a friendly squeeze. "What a horrible outlook."

"Spend two decades in captivity and see how cheerful your outlook is," Ezriah rebutted. "I must have done something really rotten when I was young to get the Almighty so mad at me."

"That's plain silly," Evelyn said.

"Is it? I used to pluck the wings off flies for the fun of it. I liked to collect ants and pour them onto a fire. I'd catch frogs and toads and lizards and cut them open just to see what was inside."

Nate was marking the progress of the clouds. "All boys pull stupid stunts like that," he commented. "My brother liked to tie cats and dogs together and watch them fight."

"What about you?" Ezriah asked. "What terrible deeds did you do?"

"Once, on my uncle's farm, I threw a rock and killed one of his geese. I was only trying to stop it from pecking me but I hit it in the head."

Ezriah's good eye squinted at him. "You call that a vile deed? Didn't you ever kill anything for the hell of it? Just to watch it die?"

"Why would I want to do that?"

The trapper chuckled. "I knew it. I knew you were one of those kids who always kept his room tidy and never gave his folks a lick of sass."

"Hardly," Nate said. As he recollected, he was forever in trouble with his father, as harsh a taskmaster as ever lived. A man not averse to applying a hickory switch whenever the occasion demanded, and the occasions had demanded it a lot.

"My brother likes to kill things," Evelyn remarked.

"He does?" Ezriah's interest was perked. "What kind of things?"

"People."

"No fooling?"

Winona took it on herself to clarify her daughter's statement. "Stalking Coyote has counted many coup and wants to count many more. He wants to be a Shoshone leader one day."

The clouds began to drift across the glowing face on high, and Nate unfolded. "Enough chitchat. We need to reach the woods before the moon comes out again."

Grunting, Ezriah slowly rose. "I feel a little better," he said.

They crept into the tall grass. The wind had intensified, and the stems swayed and rustled, lending the illusion they were moving through a living sea.

Stygian blackness descended, just as Nate anticipated. "Hold hands," he directed, so they wouldn't stray apart. He grasped Winona's wrist.

To the northwest the wavering howl of a lone wolf echoed off the peaks. The wolf was answered by another. Distorted by distance, the cry ululated eerily like the otherworldly wail of a demon.

Ezriah was keeping up. But when they were halfway across he called out softly, "Can we go a mite slower? Remember, I'm not as young as the rest of you."

"It is all that gold," Winona said. "It must weigh as much as Evelyn does."

"More," Ezriah said. "But if you think I'll leave it behind, you're a loon." He wrapped his free arm around the leather bag. "The only way I'll give it up is if someone pries it from my cold, dead fingers."

"You can be morbid sometimes, Ezriah," Winona whispered.

"I can?" The trapper was quiet several seconds. "Is that good or bad?"

The wolfish howls faded. Nate became aware the clouds were scuttling across the sky faster than he foresaw. The moon would emerge well before they reached the sheltering woods.

Then the howls resumed, but with a new note to them, a tremulous, throaty quality that brought Nate to a sudden halt. His pulse leaped as he gazed toward Huntington Manor. Their luck had just run out.

"What is it, Pa?" Evelyn wanted to know.

"The bloodhounds are after us."

Chapter Nine

A mental image of his daughter and his wife being ripped to bits by eight slavering, snarling beasts galvanized Nate King into crying, "Run! Run for the trees!" The urging was scarcely needed. Winona and Evelyn had already broken into a run. Ezriah Hampton clutched his leather bag in both arms and followed suit.

Nate brought up the rear, his mind racing faster than his feet. They had five minutes, maybe a few more, before the bloodhounds caught up. Eluding the brutes was next to impossible, thanks to their phenomenal sense of smell. Shooting them was best, but he and Winona would only be able to pick a few off before the rest tore into them. As a last resort, climbing trees would put them out of the pack's reach, but the dogs would stay at the bottom, baying and barking until their masters arrived.

There has to be something else we can do! Nate told himself. He refused to give up hope, refused to accept that there wasn't a way to keep the hounds from bringing them to bay. All he had to do was think of it.

Judging by the sound, the dogs had been released near the stable. Probably at the point where the scent trail led into the grass. Their pursuit would be swift, but they wouldn't run flat out until their quarry was in sight. Bloodhounds always conserved their energy for the final spurt of speed needed to bring down whatever they were after.

Winona and Evelyn reached the woodland. Ezriah huffed in after them, tottering as if drunk, his pale features slick with perspiration.

Pausing, Winona asked, "Which way, husband?" She had no experience with dogs and was depending on him to save them.

Nate surveyed the vegetation, which was mired in murk. But it might as well be noon for all the good the darkness did them. Night or day was of no consequence to bloodhounds. They relied on their noses, not their eyes.

Their noses. Nate selected one of the thickest, tallest pines, and pointed. "I want Evelyn and you to climb. Keep close to the trunk, and whatever you do, don't move or speak. Not even to whisper to one another."

Without hesitation Winona turned to do as he had bid her. "I will boost you up, Blue Flower."

"First I need your possibles bag," Nate said.

Again Winona didn't question his judgment. She slid it over her head and handed it to him.

Nate indicated another tree. "That one is yours," he said to Hampton. "Get up there and don't let out a peep."

Ezriah was struggling to regain his breath. "Did you get hit on the noggin when I wasn't looking? The damn dogs will trap us up there until the soldier boys show up. It's plain stupid."

"Trust me," Nate urgently coaxed. "I have a plan. And for it to work, I need your cloak."

"What in tarnation for?"

"I need something with your scent on it," Nate said. "How about your hat instead? Or that leather bag you're so powerful fond of?"

"The cloak it is." Ezriah put down the bag and hastily removed the garment. "I hope I get this back. I've grown quite attached to it."

"Get up the tree," Nate directed.

Ezriah set a condition. "Only if you pass my gold up to me."

Nate set a condition of his own, annoyed the man could quibble when their lives hung in the balance. "Only if you hurry."

Ezriah gripped a low limb and started to pull himself up but he was much too slow. Nate gripped the older man's spindly legs and catapulted him upward. Squawking, Ezriah clung to the bole for dear life, the Kentucky in the crook of his left elbow.

"Warn a fella next time, will you? I nearly cracked my skull!"

Nate wasted no time in hoisting the heavy bag overhead. The trapper grunted as he grabbed hold, and pulled it up beside him with an effort.

"You'll have to climb higher," Nate advised, "to where the limbs are thickest. Make yourself as comfortable as you can because I don't know how long it will be before you can come back down."

"And where will you be while the rest of us are pretending we're squirrels?" Ezriah demanded.

"Trying to throw the dogs off our scent." Nate turned. His wife and daughter were looking down at him, their anxiety transparent. "No matter what you hear, you're to stay up there until I say the coast is clear. Is that understood?"

"If we hear you are in trouble, we will come help you," Winona said.

"You'd do the same for us, Pa," Evelyn declared.

Arguing was pointless. "Get a lot higher," Nate reiterated, and ran northward. Twisting and bending low, he dragged Ezriah's cloak and Winona's possibles bag beside him, mingling their scent with his in an attempt to dupe the bloodhounds into thinking the four of them were still together. Evelyn's scent was missing, but Nate hoped the dogs wouldn't notice in the rush of the moment.

The braying had increased in volume. Confident in their ability, in their infallible sense of smell, the pack was rapidly narrowing the gap.

Nate zigzagged to make it harder. He circled random trees and bushes, he deliberately went up over logs and small boulders, he did anything and everything he could to temporarily confuse them. He waited until their racket convinced him they were almost to the woodland, and then cast about for a suitable tree for himself. A tall spruce was ideal.

Running past it another twenty yards, Nate balled up Winona's possibles bag inside Ezriah's cloak and threw both five or six yards into a thicket. Then he pivoted and raced back to the spruce. It was about seven feet from the scent trail. Coiling, he leaped with all the strength his sinews could muster, his right arm forking a limb that sagged under his weight but didn't break. Holding on, he wrapped his leg around another branch and levered upward, the Hawken in his left hand. Climbing with it was awkward but he wasn't about to cast it aside.

The crackle of brush told Nate the bloodhounds were in among the trees. The moment of truth had arrived. Would the dogs keep on coming, fooled by the parfleche and the cloak, or would they realize that three of those they were after had taken refuge in nearby pines? With bated breath Nate listened intently, his heart leaping into his throat when he thought he heard the pack milling about as if they had tumbled to the deception. Then one of the bloodhounds brayed louder than the rest and there was a tremendous din as they hurtled northward again, the tenor of their cries proof they anticipated a quick end to the chase.

Nate had climbed some twenty-five feet. Pressing against the trunk, his cheek flush, he wedged the Hawken between his chest and the bark.

Out of the darkness they came, eight loping shapes, their heads down, their tails high, the keening of their howls rising to a feverish pitch. They streaked past the spruce to where Nate had discarded the cloak—and abruptly stopped dead as if they had run into an invisible wall. A new note, one of confusion and urgency, entered their voices as they frantically roved about seeking more scent. Some lifted their great heads and yipped in plaintive dismay.

Inwardly, Nate smiled. So far, so good.

The thunder of hooves announced the arrival of the militiamen, seven of them with Colonel Proctor at their head. They plowed through the brush and reined up amid the milling dogs, the colonel blurting, "What the hell? They've lost the scent!"

"How can that be?" Sergeant Braddock said. "King and the others can't just crawl into a hole and pull the dirt in after them."

"They have to be around here somewhere, sir." This from Private Yates.

"And we're going to find them!" Colonel Proctor snarled. "Yates, I want Timmons and you to leash the dogs and backtrack. The rest of you men, stay alert! They might intend to ambush us."

Yates and Timmons dismounted and gave the reins of their mounts to Private Danvers. Braddock, Mitchell, and Stewart covered the pair with rifles as they gathered up the madly sniffing hounds and secured them, four to a leash.

The dogs were superbly trained. As soon as they were in harness, they stopped milling and looked to their handlers for instructions. Yates and Timmons headed them back down the scent trail.

Nate shifted and grasped the Hawken in both hands. Peering through the branches, he watched as the bloodhounds were set to looking for a trail that diverged from the one he had made. The riders were scouring the undergrowth, and every now and again one or the other would gaze up into the trees. Nate was glad they hadn't thought to bring a torch along.

Scarcely had the thought crossed his mind when light flared, and Private Mitchell held a crackling brand aloft.

"Look for sign!" Colonel Proctor thundered. "Crushed grass, broken bushes, footprints, anything!"

The torch neared the spot where Nate had left his loved ones and Ezriah Hampton. Straining at their leashes, the dogs were sniffing nonstop.

Nate rested the Hawken's barrel on an adjacent limb and sighted on Mitchell's head. If he had to, he would draw their fire to lure them away from Winona and Evelyn.

"The dogs are stumped, sir," Private Yates reported.

"It's as if the mountain man and his bunch vanished into thin air, sir," Private Timmons said.

"Spare me your worthless insights," Colonel Proctor responded. "I want results, gentlemen! The Kings must suffer for the indignity they had heaped on me. I offered them the hospitality of my home, I gave them a chance to contribute to the glory of New Eden, and they spurned both. They assaulted two of you, they hurt sweet Harriet. They even had the sheer audacity to kill one of my prized bloodhounds!"

"And they shot Rufus, sir," Sergeant Braddock reminded him.

"Stable hands are expendable, Sergeant. Purebred bloodhounds are not."

Private Mitchell had a comment to interject. "Rufus said it was the squaw who shot him, sir. She was the one who shot Young Blue, too."

"I hear tell squaws are bloodthirsty bitches," Private Stewart said. "What sort of man marries one, anyway?"

"A vicious viper," Colonel Proctor said. "All Indians are savages, and whites who live like them are little better. Mountain men are outcasts, the flotsam and jetsam of society. They can't make a go of it in the white world so they forsake their heritage and adopt red ways."

"Nate King was always civil to me, sir," Sergeant Braddock had the courage to remark. "And his family struck me as decent enough."

"They pulled the wool over your eyes, Sergeant," the colonel said. "A grizzly cub is still a grizzly, is it not? A she-bear will tear you to shreds the same as a male, will she not? Don't let their civility fool you. Given half a chance, any one of them would have stuck a knife in your ribs."

"Even the little girl, sir?"

"Especially the child. She's the most deceptive of all." Colonel Proctor had to firm his hold on the reins of his stallion, which did not like being so close to the hounds. "Maggots come in all sizes, Sergeant. Small or big, they deserve to be crushed underfoot."

"So you planned all along to kill them eventually?" Sergeant Braddock asked.

"We couldn't very well hold them against their will and then later let them go, now, could we?" Proctor rejoined. "They'd tell others and bring unnecessary grief down on our heads."

David Thompson

"So you did plan to kill them?" Sergeant Braddock persisted.

Proctor was evasive. "Who can say? The woman is a marvelous linguist and I need an interpreter. As for her husband, it would depend on whether he saw the light and agreed to help us of his own free will." Proctor paused. "Enough pointless questions! All of you, concentrate on the task at hand."

Nate's hatred of the colonel surged to new heights. The man was pure evil; Proctor manipulated others as if they were pieces on a chessboard. Everything had to be done exactly as he wanted, no dissent allowed. Were Proctor ever to be elected governor of New Eden, he would rule with an iron fist, a virtual dictator, his only goal to satisfy his lust for power. There would be no end to his self-serving, wicked deeds.

Yates and four of the bloodhounds were near the tree in which Winona and Evelyn were roosting. Nate couldn't see them from where he was, and he prayed none of the militiamen could, either.

"Maybe this is the squaw's work again, sir," Private Yates commented. "Maybe Injuns have a trick for throwing wolves and such off their scent, and the squaw used it on your dogs. Maybe that's why they're acting so confused."

"I wouldn't put anything past one of those heathens, sir," Private Mitchell said. "Man or woman."

"Which is why establishing a truce is so essential," Colonel Proctor said. "It will give our militia time to grow to where we can wipe out the surrounding tribes village by village without hindrance. Think of it! A couple of hundred men armed with the latest military ordnance! We'll be unstoppable."

It was no idle boast, Nate mused. Few Indians had guns. In a pitched battle they would be at a hopeless disadvantage, particularly if they were defending their families and couldn't employ their warhorses effectively. Mobility was their greatest asset; without it they would be mowed down in droves.

Nate started. Proctor and company were coming toward him again. The bloodhounds were out in front tugging at their leashes, on the same scent trail but sniffing along the edges for new spoor. Braddock and the others were spread out to the rear.

"If we don't find them tonight, we can always take up the hunt tomorrow at first light, sir," the noncom said.

"We're not giving up until they're caught," Colonel Proctor snapped. "The woman and child will be clamped in irons. As for King and that doddering old fool who is with them, I intend to make an example of both."

"You intend to put the little girl in shackles, sir?" Sergeant Braddock said.

The colonel glanced sharply at his subordinate. "I don't like your tone, Sergeant. You're beginning to worry me. In case you've forgotten, the future of New Eden is at stake. And, need I also remind you, so is the future of your own families."

"But Evelyn King is so young—"

"I had no idea you were this tenderhearted, Sergeant. It's unbecoming in a soldier. Duty before all else, remember? Age is of no consequence in time of war, and make no mistake, we are in a state of perpetual war until such time as we have subdued all the tribes within five hundred miles of New Eden."

"I don't believe in making war on children, sir," Sergeant Braddock said.

"Enough!" Colonel Proctor fumed. "Your whining grows tiresome. A professional military man must learn to set his personal feelings aside to serve the higher good."

Yates and Timmons had reached the spot where the trail ended. Once again the bloodhounds were stymied and roved about sniffing and whining.

Colonel Proctor swore a blue streak. "The best hunting dogs in North Carolina, outwitted by a mountain man and his squaw!"

"They're out of practice, sir," Private Yates said. "It's been months since we took them out hunting so much as a rabbit."

"It's my fault, I suppose," Colonel Proctor said. "This is what I reap for devoting too much time to the establishment of our settlement."

"You can't fault yourself alone, sir," Private Stewart responded. "We've all been too busy."

"Thank you, Private, but just as I won't accept excuses from any of you for a job you perform poorly, I won't accept excuses for my own shortcomings. We must all be man enough to accept responsibility when we've erred." Proctor stared at the dogs. "It's time to change tactics. Start nosing them into every thicket and around every tree. There has to be some trace of King and his family. There simply has to be."

Nate saw Yates guide four of the dogs toward the base of the spruce. Tensing, he angled the Hawken downward and rested his thumb on the hammer.

Suddenly Sergeant Braddock called out, "Sir! What's that to the north!"

Everyone looked, including Private Yates, who halted and glanced over his shoulder.

Nate had to crane past the trunk to see. On the slope of a mountain bordering the valley glowed a point of light no bigger than the head of a pin.

"It's a campfire," Colonel Proctor said. "Perhaps it's Lame Bear, on his way back to us. If so, he should be here by early tomorrow afternoon."

Private Danvers extended an arm. "If it is him, sir, he's brought company. Take a gander about half a mile to the west of the campfire. What do you see?"

Another light, Nate discovered. *Another campfire.* Not only that, but from his elevated position he could see what was hidden to those below, to the east of the others. Three camps betokened a large party that had split into thirds. The scarcity of whites in the region virtually insured that they were Indians, and the number involved did not bode well for the people of New Eden. His conclusion was partly shared by the colonel.

"I suspect they are Indians, gentlemen. Lots and lots of Indians."

"Waiting until dawn to come down into the valley," Sergeant Braddock said. "The question is, what will they do when they get here? Are they a friendly tribe or a war party of hostiles?"

"We can ill afford to make assumptions either way," Colonel Proctor said. "For the nonce we must break off the hunt and return to Huntington Manor. Everyone else must be warned, and a suitable reception arranged. If our visitors prove unfriendly, they'll wish they had let us be."

"Do you suppose the Kings were right?" Sergeant Braddock said. "Maybe sending Lame Bear out has let the wrong tribes know where we are."

"We'll know soon enough." Proctor reined his stallion around. "I hate giving up but New Eden takes priority. Timmons, Yates, on your horses. It's late and we have a lot to do before dawn."

The militiamen formed into a column of twos, Yates assigned to handle the bloodhounds. At a signal from the officer they departed at a trot.

Nate started down before they were out of sight, reclaimed the cloak and possibles bag, and hastened to where he had left the others.

"Winona! Evelyn! You can come down now!"

"Is that you, Pa?"

"No, it's William Proctor," Nate teased.

From the tree to his left floated an irate query. "What about me, hoss? Or are you hoping I'll sit up here until hell freezes over?"

"Look to the north, Ezriah."

127

"The north? What the blazes for? What's there that—" Hampton was quiet for all of ten seconds. "Damnation. Tomorrow this valley will be crawling with the devils. We'd best forget about getting any sleep tonight and light a shuck."

Nate's thinking, exactly. If they headed out right away, they could be through the pass to the south by daybreak, or shortly thereafter. Then it was on to Bent's Fort to relay word to the proper authorities about the colonel's plans. Surely, Nate reasoned, the government wouldn't stand idly by while a power-hungry lunatic waged a one-man war against every tribe in the Rockies.

Winona swung to earth as lithely as a cougar. She'd had a few anxious minutes earlier when the militiamen prowled about below the tree. The entire time, she had trained her rifle on Proctor, ready to send a ball squarely between his eyes if the soldiers spotted Evelyn and her.

Just then her daughter lowered herself onto the final branch. "Want me to jump, Ma?"

"No, I will catch you." Winona leaned her Hawken against the trunk and stretched her arms upward.

Giggling, Evelyn dropped without hesitation. As she was lowered to the grass she remarked, "That was fun. I like climbing trees."

"So did I when I was your age," Winona said. The ability of children to make the most of every situation never ceased to amaze her. Here they were, fleeing for their lives, and Blue Flower was treating it as a lark.

Nate moved under the tree the trapper had scaled. Hampton was descending with all the speed of petrified molasses, and a lot of grunting and muttering. "Are you all right up there?" Nate asked.

"Why wouldn't I be?" Ezriah said sourly. "Because I get poked and scratched every time I move? Because I about had my eye gouged out? Because these old bones aren't as limber as they once were?"

"You're alive, aren't you?"

"Why is it you keep bringing that up whenever I gripe? If I fell off a cliff and was all busted up but still breathing, I bet you'd walk up and say, 'But you're still alive. What are you complaining about?'"

Nate chuckled at how accurately Ezriah mimicked him. "I probably would at that," he conceded. He could see the oldster now, ten feet up and gingerly feeling his way lower limb by limb.

Winona brought Evelyn over. "I take it, husband, you saw the fires in the mountains?" she inquired. She had spotted them as soon as she climbed up. "I sincerely doubt they are Flatheads or Nez Perce."

"Or Crows," Nate said.

"Then you know what that means. And you heard Proctor. His people will be busy the rest of the night preparing for an attack. We can slip through to the pass and be gone before they know it." As happy as the prospect made her, Winona was concerned for Thomas. If the settlement was attacked, he would suffer the same fate as the whites.

"At the rate Mr. Hampton is going, we won't get to leave here until dawn," Evelyn playfully commented.

From above them came a snort. "I heard that, girl! I'd like to see you do half as well when you're half my age."

"When you get a little lower, do like I did and jump," Evelyn suggested. "My pa will catch you."

"I will?" Nate said.

"I'll do it my own self, thank you very much," Ezriah grumbled. "Your butterfingers of a father might drop me."

Presently the trapper gained the lowest limb, and hesitated. "Take my rifle and the bag, will you?"

Nate idly reached up but the heavy bag slipped. He grabbed

at the strap and missed. With a pronounced *thud* the heavy bag hit the earth, the coins jangling noisily.

"See what I meant?" Ezriah said to Evelyn.

Nate stepped aside so the trapper could shimmy down. Once Hampton had reclaimed the Kentucky and his precious gold, they filed out into the high grass. Torches flickered off near the manor and down at the stables, and figures were moving about.

Ezriah slung the bag over his shoulder. "I can't say I'm sorry to see the last of those yacks."

"Who says you have?" Sergeant Braddock inquired, unexpectedly rising up out of the grass with his rifle leveled. Instantly, four other militiamen did the same. "The colonel sends his compliments. He knew the four of you had to be close by, so he had us jump down and lie low until you showed yourselves. So what will it be? Do you drop your weapons, or do you die?"

Chapter Ten

Nate King was a volcano on the verge of erupting. He seethed with suppressed fury as he paced the bedroom again and again and again, all thoughts of sleep banished, all weariness eclipsed by the resentment that boiled within him. For the hundredth time he halted in front of the bedroom door and pounded it with a fist. "I demand to see Proctor! Bring him here, damn you!"

"Keep that up, hoss, and you're liable to pop a vein. I knew a fella who did that once. Real excitable cuss. Something burst in his head and he was never the same. Sat around staring at the walls all day, and drooling. Downright pitiful."

Nate swung toward the bed. Ezriah Hampton was on his back, his hands propped under his head. "They have my wife. They have my daughter. And you expect me to stay calm?"

"No. I'm just saying it's best if you simmer down. There's nothing we can do about it at the moment."

Nate recalled how Sergeant Braddock and the militiamen had brought them back to Huntington Manor. He had expected to be taken before the colonel, but instead Braddock brought them to the west wing and separated them. Winona and Evelyn had been placed in one room, Ezriah and he in another. That had been hours ago. Striding to the window, Nate parted the curtains. Outside, Private Danvers was standing guard, and smirked at him. "It will be daylight in half an hour."

"And we ain't had a lick of sleep all night," the trapper said. "Not good, not good at all. We need to get some rest."

"Don't let me stop you," Nate said through clenched teeth.

Ezriah sat up. "Listen, I'm as upset about the state of affairs as you are. Yes, I'm worried about your missus and the sprout. But I doubt Proctor will harm them. Put them in irons maybe, but he'll keep them alive until you come up with a way to sneak us all out of here."

Easier said than done, Nate reflected. With a guard in the hallway and a guard outside, they weren't going anywhere in the near future. In frustration he pounded his right fist into his left palm.

The clatter of hooves drew Ezriah's gaze to the window. "I wonder what they're up to out there. There sure has been a ruckus."

Nate didn't care what the settlers were up to. All that mattered were Winona and Evelyn. He resumed pacing, his emotions roiling like a pond in a tempest. It rankled him, how he had blundered into Proctor's little trap. How the colonel had outfoxed him as if he were a green pilgrim fresh off a wagon train.

Ezriah wrung his hands. "You're not the only one with worries, you know. The sons of bitches finally got around to looking in my bag and found my gold! Now Proctor has it! And we both know he'll never give it back."

"My wife and daughter are more important than your measly coins."

"Listen to yourself. And you called *me* a grump? A griz has a better disposition than you. Do yourself a favor and sit a spell."

"I can't," Nate said. The thirst for vengeance frothing deep within him had him too agitated. "I want Proctor. I want to kill him with my bare hands."

"You'd never survive as long as I did in captivity," Ezriah observed. "Twenty years I was their prisoner! I learned early on not to let my emotions get the better of me. If they do, it wears you down, makes you so miserable you're next to useless. You get so wrought up you just can't think straight."

Everything the old trapper said was true but Nate couldn't help himself. "Your wife and daughter weren't with you. It makes all the difference in the world."

"I can see where it would," Ezriah allowed, "but you're not doing them any favors by stomping around like a bull in a china shop. You need to think of a way to turn the tables on Proctor. You need to get us the hell out of this valley before those Indians swoop down and butcher everyone."

"They might be friendly," Nate said, although he didn't believe it.

"Hell, who are you trying to kid? It's the biggest damn war party you can imagine. That idiot, Proctor, never should have sent out the Crow. It was the same as sending out an engraved invite to his own massacre."

"The settlers might have a chance," Nate commented. They had plenty of guns, plenty of ammunition, plenty of supplies, and they could fortify themselves in the manor.

"There you go again. Grasping at straws. Oh, sure, maybe they can hold their own for a good long while. But eventually the warriors will wear them down and slaughter every last man, woman, and child."

Nate stepped to the door and raised his fist to pound it again, then thought better of the idea and continued to pace.

"You're learning, sonny," Ezriah said, chuckling. "If you need to pound something, pound Proctor when you get the chance."

As if in response, the door opened and in strode the colonel. Nate immediately balled both fists and started toward him, only to stop cold when Yates and Bell entered with cocked pistols.

"Back off, mountain man," the former warned. "Lay a finger on the colonel and we'll blow out your wick."

Sergeant Braddock came in last, and shut the door. "No need for threats, Private. I'm sure our guest has guessed as much."

"Guest, hell!" Nate grated. "I'm your prisoner."

Colonel Proctor moved to the oak chair and sat. "You have an excellent grasp of the situation, Mr. King. Now suppose you calm yourself so we can discuss it like two intelligent, mature adults?"

Nate's fingers twitched in impotent outrage. "I want to see Winona and Evelyn, you bastard."

"In due time, perhaps. And only if you behave yourself." Proctor aligned one of the medals on his coat. "If you don't, well . . ." He shrugged. "Unlike your wife, you're expendable. Cross me and you will never set eyes on them again."

"I overheard what you said in the woods last night," Nate responded. "You don't intend to let me live even if I do cooperate."

"Heard that, did you? More's the pity." Proctor sighed. "But I'm not ready to have you slain just yet. Obey me, and you live a little longer And if that's not enough incentive, keep in mind the suffering I can inflict on your wife and charming daughter should you refuse. Your cooperation insures they will be treated decently."

Nate made a silent vow to himself. Somehow, some way, he was going to kill William Harrison Proctor.

"Now then, shall we get down to business? First, let me thank you for the invaluable service you've rendered us."

"I've helped you?" It was the last thing Nate wanted to do. "How?"

"By escaping. Had you not run off, we wouldn't have spotted the campfires. We'd have no idea savages were gathering en masse. They'd have caught us completely by surprise. If they're hostile—"

Ezriah cackled. "There's no 'if' about it, mister. They're out for your blood, all right. Take my advice and skedaddle. Pack whatever you can carry and get the hell out of this valley."

"Run from a band of heathen dimwits?" Proctor said. "I think not. I have my pride to think of."

"Pride goeth before a fall," Ezriah quoted.

"So I've heard. But in this instance my men and I will prove equal to the occasion." Proctor grew thoughtful. "Even if I wanted to abandon New Eden, I couldn't. We don't have enough horses for everyone, and the wagons aren't due back for another month. The savages would overtake us long before we reached the pass. We'd be caught out in the open, at their mercy."

"So you're fixing to dig in and make a stand? Twelve men against a small army of redskins?"

"We don't know how many savages there are," Colonel Proctor said. "And our own strength is considerably more than you give us credit for. All the women have been trained in the use of firearms. Seven of the children are in their teens and can handle a rifle reasonably well. Another five or six can be counted on if need be. Plus the servants. That gives us close to forty-five guns. Enough, I should think, to hold off a red horde."

"Forty-five or a hundred and five, it won't make a lick of difference if those Injuns are who I think they are," Ezriah said.

"You make it sound as if the outcome is foreordained," Proctor said. "Nothing could be further from the truth. I have a few tricks up my sleeve that will win the day for us."

"That confident, are you?" Ezriah said. "So was a gent named Goliath, and look at what happened to him."

"Your biblical analogy is more apt than you realize. Goliath was bigger, stronger, better armed. Yet one stone from David's slingshot brought him low. Skill prevailed over brute force, just as our military skill will prevail over the sheer numbers of our adversaries." Colonel Proctor faced Nate. "Now where were we? Oh, yes, I'd thanked you for your inadvertent aid. It's time for you to render additional help."

"If I refuse?"

"You try my patience, sir. We have been over this already. If you decline, I will have one of my men take a bullwhip to your wife."

Nate couldn't help himself. He reached Proctor in two leaps and wrapped his fingers around the man's thick neck. But as he started to squeeze, the potential consequences to Winona and Evelyn stopped him. That, and the pistol shoved against his ribs.

"Let go of the colonel!" Private Yates growled.

Slowly uncurling his fingers, Nate stepped back. His temples were pounding so loudly he barely heard Proctor.

"That's better. You're being reasonable. I'll reciprocate and not punish your wife for your stupidity." Proctor smoothed his jacket. "A horse is being saddled at the stable. As soon as the sun rises, you will mount up and ride north. Scout out the Indians. Find out who they are, how many there are, and what they are up to. You should be able to accomplish all that and be back here by the middle of the afternoon."

"I'm to go unarmed, I gather?"

"Need you ask? Rely on stealth and caution instead."

"What about me?" Ezriah asked.

"You, sir, are next to worthless. I would have you taken out and shot, except I'm not one to needlessly squander resources, however feeble they are. There may yet be some use I can put you to." Colonel Proctor rose. "Sergeant Braddock will be back for you shortly," he told Nate. "If you're smart, you won't give him any trouble."

The officer and militiamen left. Nate, bowing his head, slumped into the chair the Southerner had vacated.

"Don't take it so hard, hoss," Ezriah said. "You've got to learn to look at the bright side of things. Every cloud has its silver lining."

"And there's one here I've overlooked? Talk sense. We're at Proctor's mercy and there's nothing we can do about it."

Ezriah slid to the end of the bed. "Listen to yourself. Why don't you just curl up and die so I won't have to watch you mope?" He gestured. "In a little while Proctor is cutting you loose to spy for him. You'll be on your own, able to do whatever you want. A savvy coon like you can turn that to his advantage, I'm thinking."

Now that Nate thought about it, he agreed. For starters, he could get his hands on a weapon. A knife, maybe, or a tomahawk.

"Proctor ain't the genius he thinks he is. We outsmarted him once, we can outsmart him again. Just don't give up hope."

Nate looked at the old trapper. "Thank you, Ezriah."

"Don't get all misty-eyed on me. I'm doing this for my own good as well as yours. I can't escape by myself. So I need you to stay as sharp as a Bowie."

After that the minutes dragged as if weighted down by millstones. Gradually the light beyond the curtains brightened. Nate rose when the latch rasped.

"It's time," Sergeant Braddock said. He was alone, and he hadn't drawn his pistol. "I'll take you to the stable."

"Any chance I can see Winona and Evelyn before I go?"

"No. I'm sorry. Were it up to me, I'd let you, but the colonel gave specific instructions to that effect."

"Figures."

Nate followed him into the hallway and left toward the parlor. Settlers were bustling about like bees in a hive. Luther Carson had a keg of black powder on each brawny shoulder and was about to add them to a stack against the wall. Mrs. Bell and her children were carrying foodstuffs and spare blankets toward the east wing. Others were engaged in stockpiling sundry other essentials.

"We're getting ready to go to war," Braddock said.

"You're getting ready to die."

Braddock's handsome countenance curved in a frown. "Quit that talk. I have a wife and two kids of my own, remember? I wouldn't stay on if I seriously thought they were in any great danger."

"Have you ever fought Indians before?"

"Some renegades once. They raided a couple of cabins in our county. Our company was ordered into the field and we chased them deep into the hills. Harried them so they couldn't rest, couldn't eat. They didn't put up much of a fight at the end."

"Then you have no idea what you're in store for," Nate said. Of all the militiamen, Braddock was the only one who had shown consideration for his family, and the only one who might be willing to listen to reason. "Get out while you can."

The sergeant ushered him down the front hall and out into the rosy glow of the new day. Turning, Nate scanned the windows in the hope of seeing Winona or Evelyn.

"They're on the other side," Braddock said, and lowered his voice. "I'm sorry about this, Nate. I like you, and I don't agree with how the colonel is treating you. But there's nothing I can do."

"You can stand up to him. You can take command. You can order New Eden abandoned."

"On what grounds? Your say-so that we're all doomed?"

"Forget the Indians for a moment. Think about my wife, my daughter. You know what Proctor plans to do. Are you going to stand by and do nothing while he has them murdered?"

"When it comes right down to it, I don't believe he really will. I know him better than you. At heart the colonel is an honorable man."

"Is he? Or are you imagining a reflection of yourself in him?"

Nate saw Private Latham over by the stable, in front of the wide double doors, holding the reins to a saddled bay. Farther east the blazing sun was perched on the rim of the world, painting the sky in vivid hues of pink, yellow, and orange. To the south a rooster crowed.

"The colonel was just letting off steam," Braddock said. "He's been under a tremendous strain."

"Make excuses all you want. But mark my words, Mike. There will come a time, and soon, when you will see Proctor for what he truly is. And you'll have to make the most important decision of your life."

Braddock opened his mouth to say something, then glanced to their left and clamped his mouth shut again.

Guessing why, Nate swiveled.

"I thought I would see you off," Colonel Proctor said. With him still were Privates Yates and Bell, their hands on the flintlocks at their waist. "To satisfy myself you won't do anything foolish."

"If anything happens to my wife or daughter while I'm gone—" Nate began.

Proctor held up a hand. "Such theatrics! Your woman is safe enough so long as you do as I require. Quite frankly, she has been—"

David Thompson

Now it was the colonel who was interrupted by a shout from Private Latham. "Sir! Look yonder! There's a rider coming in! I think it's Lame Bear!"

A sorrel was trotting from the north, the man astride it riding bareback, his long, loose black hair whipping in the wind. He wore buckskins and moccasins. Dark stains marked his shirt and his body had an unnatural slouch to it, while his head and arms flapped with every stride the sorrel took.

"What's wrong with the half-breed?" Private Bell asked.

Nate had a hunch he knew but he kept it to himself. The sorrel was making for the stable, its sides caked with sweat, its legs layered with dirt and grime.

"Private Latham!" Proctor hollered. "Catch that animal and bring it here!"

Latham let go of the bay and angled to intercept the sorrel, which was too exhausted to give him any trouble. As he snagged the reins, he took a step back, his hand to his throat, then regained his composure and did as he had been ordered.

"Oh, God!" Private Yates bleated. "Look at what they did to him!"

Lame Bear was dead. His eyes had been gouged out, his nose and ears cut off, and from the amount of dried blood caking his chin and neck, Nate suspected the man's tongue was also missing. His torso was pockmarked with wounds, holes made by arrows that had been pulled out, as well as a lone bullet wound high on the sternum. In addition, his fingers were gone.

"They mutilated him after they killed him," Private Bell said.

Nate set him straight. "Some of it was done before he died."

To keep Lame Bear's body on the horse, the war party had taken several steps. A trimmed tree limb had been shoved down under his shirt in back, and another had been pushed through both sleeves so that the two branches formed a crude cross. A rope had then been looped around his chest and tied to the sorrel's neck. Another rope, pulled tight underneath the animal, linked both ankles.

"They tortured him to get information," Colonel Proctor stated.

"They tortured him to test his courage, to amuse themselves," Nate said. "They had already learned what they wanted to know."

"How do you know? You weren't there."

"I know how the Indians who did this think. I know Lame Bear would have told them everything he knew before they so much as cut him."

"Speculation, pure and simple."

Sergeant Braddock cleared his throat. "One thing is for sure. Now that we know the Indians are hostile, there's no need to send out Mr. King."

Colonel Proctor disagreed. "You couldn't be more wrong, Sergeant. It's more imperative than ever he go. We must learn how large the enemy force is, and get some idea of its disposition. As a frontiersman, Mr. King is just the man to obtain that information."

"But they might do to him what they did to Lame Bear."

"Not if he's careful," Proctor said harshly. "Or would you rather take his place? Perhaps have one of the men do it?" He placed his hands on his hips. "This newfound habit you have of questioning my decisions is grating on my nerves. You've never done it in the past. Why start now?"

Nate spared the noncom from having to answer by heading toward the bay. "I'm tired of listening to you squabble. If all goes well, I should be back in four or five hours."

Yates, Bell, and Latham dashed after him, drawing their weapons, and Private Yates barked, "Hold on there! The colonel didn't say you could leave yet."

"Let him go!" Proctor commanded. "It's what I want him

to do, isn't it?" He hiked his hands heavenward. "Imbecility runs rampant again. Don't any of you use your heads for anything other than hat racks?"

"Sorry, Colonel," Private Yates said.

Nate was eager to leave but not for the reason Proctor believed. He had no intention of spying on the hostiles, not when the time could be put to wiser use in circling around and spiriting Winona, Evelyn, and Hampton out of there. Exactly how he would do it remained to be seen. Reaching the bay, he climbed on.

"One last thing," Colonel Proctor called out. "If you attempt to deceive us, I'll have your friend Ezriah staked out in the field north of the kennel for the hostiles to find. Unless you want him to end up like Lame Bear, don't try to be clever."

A flick of the reins, and Nate rode northward. Once he was past Huntington Manor he glanced back and was rewarded with a glimpse of Evelyn at a window. She beamed and waved, and he did likewise. He saw her turn and say something and a second later Winona was there, as beautiful as the day he met her. A constriction formed in his throat as she, too, smiled and waved.

"Hang on, my love," Nate said aloud even though she couldn't possibly hear him. "I'm going to free you or die trying."

Winona had been listening at the door when Evelyn yipped in pure delight. "Ma! Come quick! "It's Pa! He's riding off, and he sees me!"

Rushing to the window, Winona felt her stomach churn with anxiety. Proctor was sending her husband off to spy on the war party, as he had told her he would. It could well be the last time she saw Nate alive. Her knees weakened and she gripped a window rail for support.

"He's smiling at us!" Evelyn declared. "He doesn't look worried, so why should we be?"

Winona didn't have the heart to tell her daughter that Nate was putting on a brave front for their benefit. She watched until the bay and her man were a speck in the morning haze; then she returned to the door.

Private Stewart was out in the hall, guarding them. Winona had been listening on the off chance he would leave his post, however briefly, so she could whisk Evelyn away. But all she ever heard him do was cough. Now, though, when she put her right ear to the wood she learned he was talking to someone, someone she recognized.

Scooting to the bed, Winona sat down just as the door opened. In walked Thomas, bearing his ever-present tray laden with two plates heaped with eggs and bacon.

"Good morning, ladies. The colonel's compliments. Breakfast is served." He used his foot to close the door, then winked and whispered. "I'm sorry you didn't succeed, but I'm giddy you're alive."

Winona was at his side in a twinkling. "We need your help again."

"To escape? Land sakes, Mrs. King. You're not one to let grass grow under you. But I don't see how I can help."

"Bring me a sharp knife," Winona whispered. "I'll take care of the rest."

"I'd be only too happy to accommodate you. But the colonel is bound to figure out I was to blame. And the whipping he had the sergeant give Private Latham is nothing compared to what the colonel does to slaves who defy him."

"He will not lay a lash on you, Thomas. I give you my word."

The manservant's eyebrows met over his nose. "Why would that be, Mrs. King? Do you know something I don't?"

"Yes," Winona said. "He will not be able to whip you because you will not be here. This time we are taking you with us."

Chapter Eleven

Nate King intended to ride a mile from the manor and swing to the west in a wide loop that would bring him up on the settlement from the west. Proctor was bound to have someone watching him from an upper window, and by then he would be well out of sight and could do as he pleased. But he had only gone half a mile when his plan was foiled by an unforeseen development.

Nate had just skirted a stand of cottonwoods and was studying the mountain slopes to the north for sign of the war party when a long line of painted warriors appeared less than five hundred yards ahead. He instantly reined up but it was too late to hide. They had seen him, and a series of war whoops punctuated the air. He counted at least fifty men, all afoot. Only a few had guns.

Nate recognized them immediately. Piegans and Bloods, two of the tribes that formed the dreaded Blackfoot Confederacy. Implacable haters of the white man, they had for decades waged a war of white extermination. In recent years their power had waned somewhat, more because of disease than warfare, but they were still a formidable force to reckon with. And when they combined in a united campaign, as they had now, few enemies could withstand them.

Plainly, they had broken camp well before daylight and descended into the valley under cover of darkness. They would reach the manor in no time.

Nate wheeled the bay. In doing so he spotted another long skirmish line approaching from the northeast. Another fifty or sixty painted warriors, most in buckskins, some in breechclouts, with shields and bows and lances. He glanced to the northwest, an icy chill searing him at the sight of yet a third long line. One hundred and fifty warriors, all told. More than enough to wipe out the settlers of New Eden.

Several warriors, all holding bows, broke from the center line and raced toward him with the celerity of antelope.

Nate wasn't about to let them get within range. He spurred the bay into a gallop, streaking toward the distant buildings. Looking back as he passed the cottonwoods, he saw the bowmen were still in pursuit. A futile gesture, one that puzzled him until he happened to face around and spied a pair of husky warriors rising up out of the grass fifty feet away.

The war party had sent scouts on ahead, and now they were between him and the manor. Bending low over the saddle, Nate reined to the right. Both men were armed with bows; both had arrows nocked. One let fly and the shaft whizzed above Nate's back, missing him by a cat's whisker.

The other warrior tried to bring down the bay. He carefully sighted down an arrow, steadied his arms, and released.

Glittering death flashed toward the animal's side. Straightening, Nate hauled on the reins for all he was worth, slewing the horse sideways. The arrow buzzed by under the animal's neck, and without delay Nate got out of there, riding like the wind. Surprisingly, the warriors let him go without loosing another shaft.

Nate thought of Winona and Evelyn. Sneaking back to rescue them was no longer feasible. The war party would reach the manor before he got them out. He had to warn the settlers and pray they could fend the Bloods and Piegans off long enough for an opportunity to escape to present itself.

Nate held to a gallop the entire distance. When he came to the final stretch of open grass, a yell went up from a militiaman at the northwest corner of the manor.

It was Private Bell, and he raised his rifle as the bay bore down on him. "What are you doing back so soon?"

"Get the colonel, quickly!" Nate reined up almost on top of him. "You're in for the fight of your lives!"

Before Bell could move, the rear door opened and out hastened William Harrison Proctor, Sergeant Braddock, and Private Yates.

"What's the meaning of this?" the colonel angrily demanded. "I saw you from the window. Didn't I make my orders sufficiently clear?"

"To hell with you and your orders," Nate responded. He pointed northward. "They're on their way. One hundred and fifty warriors, painted for war. You have fifteen, maybe twenty minutes at the very most."

Proctor's eyes narrowed. "If this is some sort of childish ruse—"

"Damn you!" Nate roared. "Do you think I would make something like this up? My wife and daughter are in there! Trapped, the same as the rest of you, with no time to run, and no place to run to even if we could!"

Sergeant Braddock stepped past the bay and stared toward the end of the valley. "I see a line of men, sir. A damned long line."

Colonel Proctor's military training took over. "Sergeant,

send riders to bring in the few stragglers who haven't arrived yet. Then have all the horses placed in the stable. Tell Private Mitchell and Private Latham to take up a post in the hay loft. Along with Rufus, they are to keep the savages from making off with our mounts. Covering fire will be provided from the east end of the manor. I want rifles in every window, ample ammunition for everyone." He gestured. "What are you waiting for? On the double! Move! Move! Move!"

The noncom ran off.

Private Yates motioned at Nate. "What about the mountain man, sir?"

"You will escort Mr. King back to the room he shares with that old—" Colonel Proctor stopped and rubbed his double chin. "No, strike that order. I can't spare anyone to guard them. Every available man is needed to repel the attack." He looked at Nate. "I'm giving you the run of the manor. You, your family, and that old idiot can do as you please. But give me cause to regret my generosity and I'll have you thrown to the heathens."

Nate was off the bay and inside before they could think to stop him. Settlers were scurrying about, involved in a variety of tasks. No one paid him much mind until he came to the west hallway. Private Stewart was on guard and started to elevate his rifle.

"I wouldn't, were I you. I have the colonel's permission to be here." Nate brushed past and reached for the latch. "You'd better go report to him, by the way. We're about to be attacked."

Inside, Winona thought she was imagining things when she heard her husband's voice. She was on the bed, Evelyn's head in her lap, waiting for Thomas to return as he had promised. Not daring to trust her ears, she looked up expectantly as the door opened, then jumped to her feet so suddenly she nearly spilled her daughter onto the floor. "Grizzly Killer! What are you doing here?"

"That's a fine greeting," Nate said, embracing her warmly. Into her ear he whispered, "Bloods and Piegans. More than I've ever seen in one war party at one time. We're in for it."

Evelyn had awakened, and her joy knew no limits. "Pa! Pa!" She threw her arms around his leg. "Is everything all right? Will these people let us go now?"

"It's not up to them," Nate said, his hand on her shoulders. "We're leaving when your mother and I think the time is ripe whether they like it or not."

"We must not let them separate us again," Winona declared.

"Don't forget Mr. Hampton," Evelyn said.

"We'll get him right now." Nate took her hand and they hurried into the hall. It was deserted. Stewart was gone, and from the parlor boomed Colonel Proctor's voice, dispensing instructions. Nate opened the door to the room Hampton should have been in, and stopped in astonishment. "He's gone!"

"How can this be?" Winona was as mystified as her man. "Where can he have gotten to?"

The answer was obvious. "After his gold," Nate said. "Ezriah was listening at the door, heard Stewart leave, and has gone to get his coins."

"We must find him, husband."

Venturing back out, they moved briskly to the parlor. Settlers were crammed together like eggs in a nest, the women and older children armed with rifles and pistols. Under his portrait stood Colonel Proctor, a brace of pistols girding his middle and a sword on his left hip. Private Timmons was beside him, whispering in his ear.

"I have just been informed the savages are almost upon us. All of you will take your posts. Remember, we have plenty of ammunition, but that doesn't mean we can waste it. Don't shoot unless you are sure of your targets."

"How many Indians are there, Colonel?" Mrs. Danvers asked.

"I have no idea, madam," Proctor lied. "But rest assured that however many there are, we shall prevail. In my cellar is enough food and water to last us a month. The worst that can happen is they will lay siege to us, and all we need do is wait them out. Sooner or later they will tire and go back to their villages."

The man was wrong, he was so wrong, but Nate didn't bother to say so. Proctor would resent it and accuse him of interfering.

The settlers started to disperse, many of the women nervous but trying bravely not to show it, the younger children scared to death.

Nate moved along the wall to the portrait. "How about guns for my family and me?" he requested.

"No," Colonel Proctor said without looking at him.

"We can help."

"No."

Winona tried. "What if the war party breaks in? We insist on being allowed to defend ourselves."

Proctor turned, his jaw muscles twitching. "Insist all you want. The savages won't set one foot in Huntington Manor! Not in my home, they won't!" He stalked off toward the east wing. "Don't pester me again or I might rescind my decision to let you wander freely."

Evelyn thrust her lower lip out and clenched her fists. "He's the meanest person I've ever met!"

"Let us find Ezriah," Winona suggested.

Since their weapons and effects had been stored in the drawing room the last time, Nate made that their first stop. But neither the old trapper nor their guns were there. Only

Mrs. Danvers and her four sons, ranging in age from eight to eighteen, the older three with rifles over by the window.

"Can we help you?" Mrs. Danvers asked. She was in a rocking chair, her youngest in her lap, fear clinging to her like fog to a riverbank.

"We're looking for our friend, Mr. Hampton," Nate said from the doorway. "Have you seen him, by any chance?"

"No," Mrs. Danvers replied. She was a mousy woman whose russet hair was prematurely graying at the temples. "No one was in here when we arrived."

"Thank you," Nate said, and began to back out.

"Mr. King?"

Nate had a notion of what was coming. "Yes, ma'am?"

"You live in these mountains. Your wife is an Indian so you must know Indian ways." Mrs. Danvers paused. "What are we in for? What can we expect?" More gushed from her in a torrent. "I mean, we'll win, won't we? All our guns against bows and lances, we *have* to win, wouldn't you say? It won't be terribly difficult for us to hold them off, will it? I don't want anything to happen to my children."

"There's no predicting how it will turn out," Nate said, which was as diplomatic as he could be. The truth was, they would be lucky to get out alive. "You might want to stack some furniture against the window. If they rush it and you can't hold them back, retreat into the hallway. Only one warrior can go through this door at a time, so you should be able to bottle them in the room until help comes."

"Are they really as vicious as everyone says they are?" Mrs. Danvers timidly asked.

Nate looked her in the eyes. He was trying to spare her undue anxiety, but it wouldn't do to fill her with false confidence. "They will ask no mercy, and they will show none. If they take your sons alive, your boys will be tortured and scalped. If they take you alive, well, let's just say you might end up wishing they'd slain you."

"Oh my." Mrs. Danvers pressed her youngest to her bosom and closed her eyes. "Thank you, Mr. King," she said softly.

Nate's next stop was the dining room. Sergeant Braddock was there, doing as Nate had advised Mrs. Danvers, overseeing the piling of furniture against windows. Four of the slaves were on hand, along with Mrs. Timmons and her five children. And over against the far wall lay the eight bloodhounds, their tongues lolling.

Braddock smiled thinly. "The colonel didn't want his precious dogs hurt so he had them brought in. The latest word is that the Indians are surrounding the manor. Not all of them, though. Some drifted to the south, toward the cabins."

Mrs. Timmons overheard. "I'd like to see those red devils go near our place! Our dog will tear them apart."

Winona was enormously happy to see Thomas. He had just piled a couple of chairs in front of the farthest window on the left. "Care for some help?" she said as she came up behind him.

The manservant clasped her hand. "Mrs. King! The colonel has let you out? Will miracles never cease!" He glanced toward Braddock and whispered, "I'm awful sorry I wasn't able to get you that knife. Colonel Proctor put me to work barricading the manor."

"No apology needed, Thomas," Winona said. "We're searching for Ezriah Hampton. Have you seen him anywhere around?"

"About ten minutes ago, I think it was. Everyone was gathered in the parlor, and I saw Mr. Hampton go scurrying off down the west hall, grinning and talking to himself like he does." Thomas chuckled. "If you don't mind my saying so, he's a mighty strange man."

"None stranger," Winona said, and leaned closer. "Have

you any idea what the colonel did with our weapons?"

"Yes, ma'am. All your things are in his bedroom. But the door has a big lock and he's the only one who has a key."

The next second Harriet walked up to them, blazing with spite. "Well, look who it is! The squaw woman! I owe you for that wallop you gave me last night!" She threw back her fist to swing but Thomas stepped between them.

"That will be enough out of you, girl! Aren't there enough enemies outside for you to fight? You have to pick on a friend?"

"She might be your friend, Father," Harriet said with brittle vehemence. "She sure as hell isn't mine. Thanks to her, I didn't get to be with the colonel last night. He was upset she got the better of me."

"What else did you expect? That he'd take you into his arms and tell you how sorry he was?" Thomas seemed to age ten years before Winona's eyes. "I've told you a million times, I'll tell you again. You mean less to him than the dirt he walks on. You're his property, his slave. One of these days he'll dump you and you'll come crying to me with a broken heart."

Harriet motioned sharply. "Don't start in on me again. Not here. Not in front of her. I don't care what you say. Bill loves me. I know he does. In a year or so he'll set me free, and then—"

"And then nothing, child. It won't happen. He's been leading you on, filling your pretty head with words you want to hear."

"How can you talk about him this way?" Harriet said. "After all he's done for you over the years? I have half a mind to tell him what you really think of him."

"You do, and we'll both be thrown to the dogs."

The crack of a shot from the second floor ended their dispute. Every person in the dining room glanced up, waiting for an outcry, for some sign the war party was attacking, but a shout from above showed that wasn't the case.

"It's all right! The Stewart boy thought he saw a redskin crawling toward the manor! But it was nothing!"

Harriet gave Winona a last glare, then walked off in a huff, over to where Aletha was clearing chairs from around the long table.

"I apologize for my daughter, Mrs. King," Thomas said sorrowfully. "She's always been willful. Always insisted on living her life her way. What I say doesn't count."

"She is young yet, Thomas," Winona said. "Maybe she will learn her lesson and grow to appreciate your love." If they lived, that was.

"I surely do hope so," the manservant said. "I pray each and every night the good Lord will bring that girl to her senses. Can't say as He's answered me yet. Or maybe He's just going about it in His own special way."

Winona caught Nate looking at her. "I must go, but I will be back," she said. "Have you asked Harriet yet about coming with us?"

"No. I know what she'll say. And I'm afraid she'll run to the colonel and spoil everything for you." Thomas's shoulders slumped. "Forget about me, Mrs. King. She won't go and I won't leave her. Come what may, I'm sticking with my daughter until the end."

"We will talk more later," Winona said. She was loathe to leave but Nate was beckoning and Evelyn had already skipped over to join him. She hurried across.

"Sergeant Braddock just informed me he saw Hampton lurking at the east end of the hall a while ago."

Winona nodded. "Could well be. Thomas told me our weapons and bags were placed in Proctor's bedroom. Somehow Ezriah found out."

The corridor was empty. The majority of the settlers were scattered throughout the manor, awaiting the inevitable.

Nate tried the latch when they came to Proctor's room, and much to his surprise the door was unlocked. Looking both ways to insure that the colonel was nowhere in sight, he gingerly pushed.

The room was a shambles. It looked as if a tornado had torn through it, overturning furniture, throwing the pillows, quilt, and mattress off the bed, and scattering the contents of a closet willy-nilly.

"What in the world?" Evelyn said.

"Hampton was looking for his gold," Nate guessed. And apparently Ezriah found it, too, because the window was wide open. Wary not to expose himself, Nate leaned on the sill and peered between the curtains.

An unnatural quiet reigned over New Eden. Not so much as a bird stirred anywhere. The stable doors were closed, the corral empty. Off toward the cabins a dog barked frenziedly.

"Do you see him?" Winona asked at his side.

"No. He must have snuck off during all the confusion."

"Without us?" Winona had expected better of the oldster.

"How did he get in here, Pa?" Evelyn inquired. "Thomas said the room was supposed to be locked."

"He must have picked the lock. That old coon is trickier than we gave him credit for." Nate was strongly tempted to make a break for it while they could. Their weapons and possibles were piled in a nearby corner. The suggestion was on the tip of his tongue when movement in the high grass south of the stable betrayed several skulking forms.

"Warriors," Winona said.

"I see them." Nate also saw five or six more, to the southeast. Huntington Manor was completely encircled. "It won't be long."

Evelyn molded herself to Winona. "Do you reckon Mr. Hampton made it out without being spotted?"

"He might have," Nate said. "If he got out before the war

party tightened the noose." Stepping back, he lowered the window and worked the bolt.

Winona moved to the corner to commence rearming herself. "Colonel Proctor will have a fit if he sees us with our guns."

"I hope he tries to take them away from us," Nate said, shoving a pair of pistols under his belt. "From here on out it's do or die. If anyone gets in our way, anyone at all, don't hold back. We've gone easy on them so far. No more."

"Do I get a gun, Pa?" Evelyn said. "I like to shoot bad people as much as you do."

"You get two," Nate said, and gave her the pair of derringers. He recovered his knife and shoved it into the sheath. His tomahawk was next. In another minute he was done, and rose wearing a grim smile. Twice now he had been caught and disarmed. He would be damned if there would be a third time.

Winona was reloading the pistol she had fired in the stable. "Have either of you seen Jack and Molly Weaver? I would like to take them with us if possible."

"Come to think of it, no," Nate said. Could it be, he wondered, the Weavers had refused to come to the manor? Or had Proctor deliberately neglected to let them know the valley had been invaded?

At that moment, down the hall a man bellowed, "Fire! Fire! The heathens have set our cabins ablaze!"

Feet pounded, and yells peppered the building. Darting to the window, Nate parted the curtain. Thick columns of smoke were spiraling skyward from three of the six homesteads. As he looked on, a fourth column spewed to life.

"It has begun," Winona said, gazing over his shoulder.

A tremendous commotion rocked the manor, a bedlam of shouts and strident cries. Nate began to turn to go investigate when he saw several settlers sprinting toward the rutted road. Private Bell was in front, urging on his two sons and his wife.

Winona was horrified. "What are they doing?"

"Trying to save their cabin," Nate said.

The Bells never made it past the mercantile. Out of the grass streamed a volley of arrows, the barbed shafts arcing true. Bell and each member of his family were pierced five, six, seven times, and died in their tracks, the wife screaming in mortal terror, Bell vainly striving to bring his rifle to bear.

Nate heard the front door slam, heard Proctor fuming. To the south two more thick columns of flame and smoke were completing the destruction of the cabins.

Winona glanced at the stable and saw that the loft door was open. Private Latham had leaned out to behold the fate of the Bells. It was a grave mistake. An arrow thudded into the wood and he ducked back again.

"Let's check on the Weavers," Nate said.

The three of them got as far as the dining room. Suddenly the corridor was blocked by men advancing from the other direction. Colonel Proctor, Sergeant Braddock, and Private Danvers were as somber as undertakers. It didn't improve Proctor's disposition any when he saw they had their weapons.

"What the hell! Where did you get those?"

"Where do you think?" Nate retorted, leveling his Hawken as Private Danvers grabbed for a pistol. "Don't try it! I'll kill the first man who touches a gun."

Proctor was as smugly arrogant as ever. "There are dozens of us and only three of you. Give up while you can."

Winona fixed a bead on the center of the officer's forehead. "You no longer tell us what to do. I would shoot you where you stand were it not for all those who are depending on you to save them. It would put the women and children in a panic, and they are scared enough as it is."

Lightning crackled on Colonel Proctor's brow. "Of all the unmitigated gall! Sergeant, go get Yates, Mitchell, and Stewart. I want these upstarts disarmed and put in shackles until I decide how to dispose of them."

"No one is going anywhere," Nate said.

Proctor placed his hands on his pistols.

That was when a shrill shout from the second floor heralded the advent of hell on earth. "Here they come! The savages are attacking! The savages are attacking!"

Chapter Twelve

Huntington Manor resounded to the thunderous discharge of scores of rifles blasting simultaneously. Colonel Proctor swore and ran toward the dining room, Braddock and the private hard on his heels.

Nate and Winona King looked at each other. If they were to escape, there was no better time than in the frantic confusion of heated battle. But despite the looming peril, neither was ready to leave just yet.

"The Weavers," Nate said.

"And Thomas," Winona responded.

They ran into the dining room, into raw bedlam born of violent conflict. The settlers were firing and reloading as fast as they could to stem a fiery red tide battering against the outer walls. Above the din of guns and the screams of women and children rose a sustained chorus of fierce shrieks and bloodthirsty war whoops.

As Nate burst onto the scene, the middle window dissolved in a spray of glass slivers. Into the opening exploded half a dozen swarthy forms, some shoving at the piled furniture that barred their ingress, others unleashing shafts and lances.

Private Timmons and his family bore the brunt of the initial onslaught. His oldest son went down, impaled by a lance. His wife screeched as an arrow transfixed her abdomen, and when Timmons turned to aid her, he took a shaft high in the shoulder.

"Stop them!" Colonel Proctor cried. "Do you hear me? *Stop them!*"

Sergeant Braddock, Private Danvers, and Thomas moved to prevent the warriors from breaking through, firing, and clubbing as foes presented themselves.

Winona promptly rushed to the manservant's side. Drawing a pistol, she shot a dusky Blood who was sighting down a shaft at him.

Nate stayed where he was, the better to provide covering fire. Snapping the Hawken to his shoulder, he sent a slug through an undamaged window at a warrior outside who was about to shoot the noncom.

Another window shattered with a nerve-jangling crash. Harry, the cook, howled as feathers sprouted in the middle of his chest. Aletha banged off a shot, dropping the warrior who had dropped him, while Harriet stumbled backward in the grip of fright so potent that all she could do was scream, scream, scream.

Several painted furies hurtled into the new opening, to be met by a volley from Braddock, Danvers, Thomas, and Winona.

In the blink of an eye the remaining warriors disappeared. The Piegans and Bloods had retreated for the moment, leaving their dead and wounded.

"We beat them!" one of Timmons's boys hollered. "We drove them off!"

"No," Nate said. "They were only testing us, gauging our

strength. Reload before they attack again." From different points in the manor echoed the anguished wails and screeches of those who had lost loved ones. Just down the hall a woman blubbered hysterically.

Choking clouds of acrid gunsmoke made Winona cough as she grabbed Thomas's wrist and said so no one else would hear, "I ask you one more time. Get your daughter and come with us."

Thomas sighed. "It's useless, Mrs. King, but for you I'll try."

Harriet had backed against the left-hand wall. Her hands were to her throat and her eyes were frozen wide. She tried to speak as they approached but only uttered pitiable mewing sounds.

"Daughter, we can't stay here," Thomas said. "The Kings are offering us a chance to get out of this fix alive, and I say we take it."

"L-l-leave?" Harriet stuttered. "To where, father?"

Winona answered for him. "Out of the manor. Out of the valley. If we can break through to the south we can—"

"You're out of your mind!" Harriet declared. "We're safer in here than we would be outside. Besides, I'm not about to desert Bill." She pointed to where Proctor and Sergeant Braddock were in animated discussion.

"My poor, deluded child." Thomas turned profoundly sad eyes on Winona. "I'm sorry. I told you how it would be. Forget about me and save yourself if you can." He took her hand in his and pumped it. "This isn't farewell. We'll meet again in the next life, and I'll look forward to being your friend there, too."

Winona wished she could seize him and drag him off against his will, but she had to settle for saying, "You are a good man, Thomas."

Across the room Nate had reloaded the Hawken. With Evelyn in tow, he walked toward Proctor and the noncom. They were arguing, but over what, he couldn't say. All he heard was mention of a "last resort." Then the colonel saw him and motioned for silence.

"What do you want, King?" Proctor demanded. "I'm in no mood for more of your insolence."

"Where are the Weavers?"

"How the hell should I know?"

Sergeant Braddock had a fist clenched and looked as if he wanted to hit his superior. "You remember, sir," he said, his tone laced with bile. "Jack and Molly refused to retire to the manor when you sent Private Bell to fetch them. They told him they would rather take their chances on their own."

"Ah, yes. The fools," Proctor sneered. "By now they're both dead. Good riddance, I say. Neither was wholeheartedly committed to New Eden, so it's no great loss." He drew himself up to his full height. "And now, if you will excuse me, I need to bolster the morale of my troops."

Nate had never intentionally shot a man in the back before, but he came close as the colonel swaggered out. "All of you would be better off if he were dead."

"To think, I admired him once," Sergeant Braddock said, and gave a little shudder. "How is it we can be so blind to what is right under our nose?"

"My wife and I are leaving soon," Nate said. "We'd like you and your family to join us."

"I can't."

"The manor is a death trap. You're fighting a losing battle. The Bloods and Piegans will eventually break through your defenses, and once they're inside, the best you can hope to do is stave off the end."

"I know."

"Then why die if you don't have to?"

"Because I'm a soldier, Nate, and a soldier doesn't desert his post, ever. Because these are my people, my friends, and fellow militiamen, and if I ran out on them when they needed me most, I could never look myself in the mirror again. Because I'm a man, and I was raised to believe that a man does what he has to do even if he must sacrifice his life to do it." Braddock held out his hand. "But I thank you for your offer. Another time, another place, and we could have been fast friends."

"Damn," Nate said, shaking.

"Now get out of here. If the Indians do break in, you don't want to be anywhere near the manor when the colonel falls back on his last resort, as he calls it."

"Care to explain?"

"Trust me. You don't want to know." Braddock smiled in genuine affection and gave Nate a light push. "Go! And Godspeed."

A tiny hand tugging on Nate's sleeve drew him to the doorway. "Come on, Pa. You heard him. Ma is waiting for us."

Winona refused to look back, afraid she would tear up. "Thomas will not leave," she said. "What about the Weavers?"

"They stayed in their cabin," Nate reported.

"Then there is nothing to hold us here. Do we go out a window or one of the doors?" Winona had no preference.

"The window in Proctor's room. It's empty, so no one will try to stop us, and the window is close to the stable and the grass."

"His room it is, husband."

Moans and sobs filled the hallway, most issuing from the parlor, and the woman who had been blubbering hysterically was still doing so, only louder. There was so much noise that when Nate stopped at Proctor's room, he almost didn't hear the subdued murmur of voices within. Voices speaking in the Piegan tongue.

Clamping a hand over Evelyn's mouth to forestall her giving them away, Nate nodded at Winona, then at the door.

Winona put her ear to it. She wasn't conversant with the Piegan language, so all she could determine was that at least three warriors were inside. The voice of one indicated he was just on the other side.

Suddenly the latch jiggled.

Nate figured the warriors had broken in through the window during the attack and been unable to go any farther. The Piegans lived in hide lodges. They had no knowledge of hardwood doors and had never seen a latch in their life. To them, the door must have seemed to be part of the wall, and the latch must have been as alien as a Piegan lodge would be to an Easterner. But now one of their number was trying to find a way out.

Moving Evelyn several feet away, Nate handed the Hawken to her and drew two flintlocks. At short range pistols were always better to use; they were less cumbersome and could be employed in tight spaces.

Winona leaned her rifle against the wall, then palmed her pistols. Cocking the hammers, she braced herself.

The latch jiggled again, and a third time, and the door abruptly opened to reveal a startled Piegan holding a war club. Behind him were four others.

Nate and the first man locked eyes, and Nate shot him in the sternum. The warrior keeled backward but was immediately shoved forward again by his companions as they barreled out of the room. Nate took aim at a second Piegan, only to have the dead man pitch against him, throwing off his aim at the exact split second he squeezed the trigger. The ball meant for the second warrior's chest ripped into the Piegan's shoulder instead, barely slowing him down.

Winona sprang back beside Evelyn. She fired as the second warrior whirled toward them, fired again at a third Piegan who had hiked a lance to spear them.

That left two warriors—and Nate's pistols were empty. Releasing them, he whipped the doubled-edged knife from its sheath, shearing the blade upward into the forearm of the next Piegan as the man lunged with a blade of his own.

The warrior howled as his wrist was nearly severed. With remarkable rapidity, he clutched the hilt of his weapon with his other hand and flung himself forward.

Spurting blood spattered Nate's face, his eyes. Frantically blinking to clear them, he sidestepped to the left. His vision swam into focus and he saw the Piegan's blade streaking at his ribs. A twist to the side saved him but it also threw him off balance.

As the Piegan raised his blade for another stroke, a gun cracked. The slight retort of a low-caliber weapon jolted him to his knees, a small hole in his temple.

Winona, meanwhile, had her hands full with the last of their enemies. The warrior held a heavy hide shield and a war club. As she grabbed for her knife, he slammed the shield against her, battering her backward, then swung the club in an overhand blow to cave in her cranium. Stumbling, she tripped over her own feet and fell against the wall, momentarily helpless.

The warrior reared, his club sweeping high. The *pop* of a gun ended the threat he posed, his left pupil dissolving inward, and he deflated like a punctured water skin.

Winona shoved to her feet and did as her husband was doing. She stared at the smoking derringers in her daughter's small hands.

"You saved our lives," Nate said in amazement.

"I couldn't let them hurt you, Pa," Evelyn said quietly.

Winona squatted and tenderly gripped her daughter's shoulders. "Are you all right, Blue Flower?"

"Yes, Ma."

"Do not be upset. You have counted coup. Not many women do. When next we visit my people, I will recount your courage, and the story of your deed this day will be told for as long as the Shoshones endure. You should feel proud."

"I should? I feel sort of sad."

Nate was reminded of the urgency of their plight by a yell from the floor above. It was Colonel Proctor.

"The savages are massing to the north and south! Be ready! Sergeant Braddock, you know what to do if we can't hold them!"

"Into the bedroom," Nate directed, scooping up his pistols and the Hawken. Shutting the door behind them, he dashed to the window and crouched. Broken glass littered the floor and both curtains were severely torn. "Reload!" he said, yanking the Hawken's ramrod from its housing.

Winona was already pouring black powder down her rifle. She saw that the stable doors had not yet been breached, and there had not been any attempt to set the stable afire. Nor would there be. Horses were invaluable to the Blackfoot Confederacy. They possessed relatively few and were always on the lookout for more. So they were saving the stable for last.

Evelyn stepped to a tattered curtain and peeked out. "Why did they set the grass on fire?" she asked.

Nate looked out. Approximately a hundred yards to the south flames leaped into the air. A red-and-orange wall was devouring the grass at a prodigious rate. "They didn't do it on purpose," was his guess. "The fire spread from one of the burning cabins."

"If it continues eastward it will cut us off," Winona said.

Grass near the manor rustled to the passage of crawling warriors. Any moment now, the Piegans and Bloods would renew the conflict. The fury of their previous attack would pale in comparison to the next.

"Is what we're doing right?" Evelyn asked.

"Right how, princess?" Nate said.

"Leaving like this. Shouldn't we stay to help? All those

ladies, all those kids, they'll be massacred, won't they? They're all going to die."

"Yes," Nate admitted. "And if we stay, we'll die with them. Would you want that? What would be the point of throwing our lives away?"

"We have done all we could," Winona said. "We warned them to leave and they refused. We told them the Blackfoot Confederacy would not stand for having a white settlement near their territory, but they would not listen."

Evelyn gnawed on her lower lip. "I just don't like running away, Ma."

Winona couldn't stop reloading to comfort her as she would have liked. "Your father and I do not like it, either, little one, but sacrificing our own lives would not do any good."

"Sometimes discretion is the better part of valor," Nate said.

"What's that mean, exactly?"

"That there's a time and a place to stand your ground and fight to your dying breath, and there's a time and a place for doing what you can to preserve your life to fight again another day." Nate reached into his ammo pouch. "If I honestly thought it would make a difference, I wouldn't be going."

"I understand, Pa. But life sure can be cruel, can't it?" Evelyn stated.

After that no one said anything until Nate had finished reloading the last of his pistols and had wedged it under his belt. He reached for the sill, then heard footsteps in the hallway and spun.

Sergeant Braddock entered, stepping over the body of a fallen Piegan. He was leading a girl of seven or eight by the hand, and his eyes were pools of moisture. "I was hoping I would still find you here," he said huskily. "My wife and I want you to do us a favor."

"Oh, God," Nate said.

"Her name is Melissa. She's our youngest. The others refuse

to go but we're not giving Melissa any choice in the matter. We have kin in North Carolina. I wrote it all down and put the paper in here." He held out a small leather pouch. "Please. I'm begging you. There's not much time and I have to get back."

Winona took the pouch when her husband hesitated. "We will look after her as if she were our own," she pledged.

"Thank you—" Sergeant Braddock said, and became too choked with emotion to go on. Bending, he embraced his bewildered daughter, kissed her on the cheek, and then fled off down the hall as if all the demons of hell were giving chase.

"Father?" the girl said.

"You're to go with us, Melissa," Winona said, grasping her hand. "This is Evelyn. She will be your new friend."

"I want my mother and father," the girl said, trying to pull loose.

Nate had half a mind to tie her up and throw her over his shoulder. Dragging the child along posed all sorts of problems. They needed their hands free to use their weapons, and now Winona was hobbled. He didn't like it, didn't like it one bit.

A war whoop slashed the stillness outside. Another echoed it to the north of Huntington Manor. It was the prelude to a fevered chorus of rampant blood lust. Up out of the grass rose the Piegans and Bloods, every last one, and with a blistering roar they rippled toward the manor like a breaker crashing on a rocky shore. Rather than dilute their assault over a wide front, they concentrated on weak spots in the manor's defenses, on breaches they had already made, on windows already broken.

Nate was appalled to see dozens of warriors converging on the shattered window in front of him. "Back! Back!" he shouted. "Into the hallway!"

Evelyn obeyed without hesitation. Winona went next, pulling Melissa after her. The girl would not stop resisting.

"Let me go! Let me go!"

A burly shape filled the window. Nate fired, the slug coring the warrior's chest. In midstride the man sprawled across the sill, the bow he had carried clattering to the floor. His body hindered those behind him, buying Nate the seconds he needed to reach the hall and slam the door shut.

"Which way?" Winona shouted to be heard above the din. Guns, screams, and curses rose in a raucous, eardrum-splitting cacophony.

Nate glanced toward the dining hall and spotted Sergeant Braddock and a Blood locked in mortal combat in the doorway. A pistol leaped into his hand of its own accord and he fired without consciously aiming. The ball took the Blood high in the cheekbone, the man folding like soggy paper.

Braddock, winded, looked at Nate, grinned, and then drew his own pistol and plunged into the dining room.

"Father!" Melissa bawled.

Fists pounded on the bedroom door. Any second, the warriors would either batter it down or tumble to the latch.

"The side door!" Nate yelled, running to the left, to a shadowed alcove where coats hung on pegs and boots lined a short bench. The outer door had been barred, but it was the work of a moment for him to remove the stout length of oak and throw it onto the bench.

Chaos and carnage gripped the manor. Screams and whoops assailed Nate's ears as he cracked the door and peered out. The east side of the mansion was clear of Indians, due, no doubt, to the fact all the ground-floor windows were along the north and south walls.

"To the corral!" Nate said. It was directly ahead, the nearest haven.

Winona took a few strides, Melissa fighting her every inch of the way. Bending, she wrapped her left arm around the child's waist, lifted Melissa off her feet, and carried her as if she were a sack of flour.

Nate backpedaled, a pistol in his right hand. He saw warriors on both sides of the mansion, but they were locked in a mammoth struggle with the defenders and so intent on forcing their way inside that none gazed in his direction.

Unmolested, they reached the corral and slipped between the horizontal rails to duck behind the posts. Winona lowered Melissa, then had to grasp her arm when the girl tried to bolt.

More and more warriors were disappearing into the manor. The whoops, the screams, the braying of the bloodhounds, and the sounds of brutal combat swelled to a pinnacle of undiluted pandemonium. Out of the front entrance burst a militiaman wielding his rifle like a club, striking right and left in abandon. Nate didn't get a good look at who it was before the man fell under a torrent of bronzed limbs.

"We must leave, now!" Winona urged.

Nodding, Nate started to rise. Only a couple of dozen Bloods and Piegans remained outdoors.

Huntington Manor suddenly heaved and convulsed as if alive, the walls and the roof seeming to expand outward as every window still intact blew with volcanic force.

"What caused that?" Evelyn asked.

Nate remembered Proctor's comment about a last resort, and Braddock's warning. He remembered the dozens of kegs of black powder. "Get down!" he shouted, and dived, bearing his wife and both girls to the ground.

An explosion occurred in the bowels of the mansion, a titanic detonation that dwarfed the first as the sun dwarfed a candle. The roof, the walls, the individual logs fractured apart at the seams as gusts of flame and smoke shot from every opening. Gargantuan gray coils spewed upward, enveloping the top of the manor as the roof buckled in upon itself and the walls splintered like so much kindling. The rumbling crash was abominably loud, the end of the world given substance and sound. It bounced off the neighboring mountains and reverberated on down the valley as if seeking to outrace itself.

Winona swore she felt the ground shake under them. Melissa was so stunned, she stopped resisting.

Only after the rumbling ceased and the rain of debris tapered off did Nate slowly rise to see what was left. The manor lay in total ruin, fire licking at some of the timbers and beams; dust and smoke swirling above all that remained of over two hundred souls. A handful of warriors were staggering northward, the sole survivors of the war party.

Winona stood and helped the girls up. "Do you think anyone survived?"

"I'll check," Nate said, and warily ventured over. Bodies and bits of bodies were strewn thick among the rubble, the sickening stench of blood and burnt flesh rising with the smoke. He did not need to look hard to confirm that every last person, attackers and besieged alike, had perished. A few minutes of inspecting the carnage was more than he could stand. Turning his back on William Harrison Proctor's folly, he announced, "We're the only ones left."

But that was not quite accurate.

Out of the stable shuffled Privates Latham and Mitchell, both too shocked to say a word. Rufus trailed them, hobbling on a crutch, tears streaking his face.

Melissa began crying. Both Winona and Evelyn bent to comfort her, but there was no stemming tears that flowed from a child's broken heart.

"Is it over, you reckon, hoss?"

Nate pivoted. Ezriah Hampton was emerging from the tall grass, the leather bag clasped to his chest. "So there you are. Yes, it's over."

The trapper solemnly regarded the devastation. "I saw the

whole thing. The next time someone tells me the Almighty is all goodness and love, I think I'll belt him in the mouth." He paused. "So what now?"

"Now we help ourselves to horses and light a shuck for home," Nate said.

"Home," Winona King wearily repeated.

They looked at each other, and in the depths of their sorrow they smiled.

WILDERNESS

#31
BLOOD KIN
DAVID THOMPSON

Growing up in the wild frontier of the Rockies, Zach King survives countless dangers, from nature and from human predators. Like his father, the legendary Nate King, Zach has learned to anticipate threats before they appear. But even Zach can't predict the danger he'll face when he travels with his fiancée to meet her family in St. Louis. He knows they'll probably look down their noses at him because he's a half breed. He's used to that by now. But he doesn't know just how far his beloved's family will go to "protect" her from marrying Zach. Some of the self-righteous relatives will stop at nothing to save the family's good name . . . even murder.

___4757-8 $3.99 US/$4.99 CAN

WILDERNESS

#28
The Quest
David Thompson

Life in the brutal wilderness of the Rockies is never easy. Danger can appear from any direction. Whether it's in the form of hostile Indians, fierce animals, or the unforgiving elements, death can surprise any unwary frontiersman. That's why Nate King and his family have mastered the fine art of survival—and learned to provide help to their friends whenever necessary. So when one of Nate's neighbors shows up at his cabin more dead than alive, frantic with worry because his wife and child had been taken by Indians, Nate doesn't hesitate for a second. He knows what he has to do—he'll find his friend's family and bring them back safely. Or die trying.

___4572-9 $3.99 US/$4.99 CAN

Dorchester Publishing Co., Inc.
P.O. Box 6640
Wayne, PA 19087-8640

Please add $1.75 for shipping and handling for the first book and $.50 for each book thereafter. NY, NYC, and PA residents, please add appropriate sales tax. No cash, stamps, or C.O.D.s. All orders shipped within 6 weeks via postal service book rate. Canadian orders require $2.00 extra postage and must be paid in U.S. dollars through a U.S. banking facility.

Name_____
Address_____
City_____State_____Zip_____
I have enclosed $_____ in payment for the checked book(s).
Payment **must** accompany all orders. ❏ Please send a free catalog.
CHECK OUT OUR WEBSITE! www.dorchesterpub.com

WILDERNESS

Fang & Claw
David Thompson

To survive in the untamed wilderness a man needs all the friends he can get. No one can battle the continual dangers on his own. Even a fearless frontiersman like Nate King needs help now and then and he's always ready to give it when it's needed. So when an elderly Shoshone warrior comes to Nate asking for help, Nate agrees to lend a hand. The old warrior knows he doesn't have long to live and he wants to die in the remote canyon where his true love was killed many years before, slain by a giant bear straight out of Shoshone myth. No Shoshone will dare accompany the old warrior, so he and Nate will brave the dreaded canyon alone. And as Nate soon learns the hard way, some legends are far better left undisturbed.

___4862-0 $3.99 US/$4.99 CAN

WILDERNESS

#25
FRONTIER MAYHEM

David Thompson

The unforgiving wilderness of the Rocky Mountains forces a boy to grow up fast, so Nate King taught his son, Zach, how to survive the constant hazards and hardships—and he taught him well. With an Indian war party on the prowl and a marauding grizzly on the loose, young Zach is about to face the test of his life, with no room for failure. But there is one danger Nate hasn't prepared Zach for—a beautiful girl with blue eyes.

___4433-1 $3.99 US/$4.99 CAN

Dorchester Publishing Co., Inc.
P.O. Box 6640
Wayne, PA 19087-8640

Please add $1.75 for shipping and handling for the first book and $.50 for each book thereafter. NY, NYC, and PA residents, please add appropriate sales tax. No cash, stamps, or C.O.D.s. All orders shipped within 6 weeks via postal service book rate. Canadian orders require $2.00 extra postage and must be paid in U.S. dollars through a U.S. banking facility.

Name_____
Address_____
City_____ State_____ Zip_____
I have enclosed $_____ in payment for the checked book(s).
Payment <u>must</u> accompany all orders. ❑ Please send a free catalog.
    CHECK OUT OUR WEBSITE! www.dorchesterpub.com